He reached out and snagged her arm, bringing her to a stop.

"We need to keep going," she said, pulling away from him.

Diesel didn't release her. "What are you running from, Reese?"

"None of your business. And who said I was running?" She jerked her arm free of his hold and glared up at him defiantly.

He cupped her face, his heart tightening. She'd been hurt. "Whatever it was, I'm sorry it happened."

She slapped his hand away. "Why should you be sorry? You didn't do it. The Taliban did it. And I swore I'd never let anyone capture me again, but it happened." She sucked in deep breaths, blowing them out through her mouth. The color was high in her cheeks and her eyes shone with moisture. "I swore," she whispered.

Diesel cursed and pulled her into his arms. "Babe, whatever they did is done. You're a wonderful person and a strong woman."

"Not strong enough," she said into his shirt, her fingers curling into his chest.

ONE INTREPID SEAL

New York Times Bestselling Author

ELLE JAMES

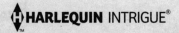

This book is dedicated to my travel buddies who make every trip
fun and exciting. Africa is on our bucket list. We hope to make
it there soon. We decided a long time ago not to wait until we
retired to travel. I'm glad we made that decision. We've been to a
lot of fun and interesting places and have so many more to visit!
If I can't get to some places, I read about them and learn.
That's the joy of books. Happy reading!

ISBN-13: 978-1-335-63914-1

One Intrepid SEAL

Copyright © 2018 by Mary Jernigan

Recycling programs
for this product may
not exist in your area.

Printed in U.S.A.

www.Harlequin.com

Elle James, a *New York Times* bestselling author, started writing when her sister challenged her to write a romance novel. She has managed a full-time job and raised three wonderful children, and she and her husband even tried ranching exotic birds (ostriches, emus and rheas). Ask her, and she'll tell you what it's like to go toe-to-toe with an angry 350-pound bird! Elle loves to hear from fans at ellejames@earthlink.net or ellejames.com.

Books by Elle James

Harlequin Intrigue

Mission: Six

One Intrepid SEAL

Ballistic Cowboys

Hot Combat
Hot Target
Hot Zone
Hot Velocity

SEAL of My Own

Navy SEAL Survival
Navy SEAL Captive
Navy SEAL to Die For
Navy SEAL Six Pack

Visit the Author Profile page at Harlequin.com.

CAST OF CHARACTERS

"Diesel" Dalton Samuel Landon—US Navy SEAL who, along with his team, is tasked to rescue a politician's son and his assistant from captivity in the Democratic Republic of the Congo.

Reese Brantley—Medically retired from active duty with the US Army, a veteran of mixed martial arts fighting and now a bodyguard for hire. On her first assignment to keep the son of a politician safe on his visit to Africa.

Ferrence Klein—Agent with the Department of Homeland Security in charge of Task Force Safe Haven.

Matthew Klein—US Secretary of Defense who hired Reese to act as Ferrence's assistant while keeping him safe.

Jean-Paul Sabando—President of the Democratic Republic of the Congo. He refused to call for democratic elections.

Laurent Sabando—Brother of the President of the Democratic Republic of the Congo. He is angry that the president turns a blind eye to what's going on with his country's natural resources.

Bosco Mutombo—Warlord determined to take over the wealth of the mines and ultimately the entire DRC.

"Pitbull" Percy Taylor—US Navy SEAL and tough guy who doesn't date much. Raised by a taciturn US Marines father. Lives by rules and structure.

Marly Simpson—Bush pilot in Africa. Her father was a navy pilot who taught her to fly. He died in a plane crash. Her mother went to work teaching children in Africa.

"Buck" Graham Bucker—US Navy SEAL and team medic. Went to medical school but didn't finish. Joined the navy and became a SEAL.

"Harm" Harmon Payne—US Navy SEAL. For a big guy, he's light on his feet and fast. Good at silent entry into buildings.

"Big Jake" Jake Schuler—US Navy SEAL and demolitions expert. Good at fine finger work.

"T-Mac" Trace McGuire—US Navy SEAL, communications man and equipment expert.

Chapter One

Reese Brantley held on to the frame of the window as the Land Rover bounced wildly over the rugged terrain. "Slow down!" she shouted to the driver.

Mubanga, the Zambian guide, seemed not to hear her. More likely, he completely ignored her as he leaned to the left to look beyond the obstruction of a pair of legs dangling over the windshield from a perch on the roof of the cab. He followed the racing leopard across the ground, heading north into the rocky hills, determinedly keeping up with the beautiful creature.

Ferrence Klein, Reese's client, who'd paid over one hundred thousand dollars for this hunting expedition, clung to his rifle from his position strapped to the top of the vehicle.

"He's not even supposed to be shooting leopards, is he? I thought there was a ban on shooting big cats? What the hell are you thinking?" Had Reese known Klein was coming to Africa to bag a leopard, she'd have told him *no way*. Her understanding was that he was there on a diplomatic mission for his father, the Secretary of Defense.

She wasn't playing bodyguard to an endangered-animal killer. If they weren't traveling so fast and furious, she'd have gotten out of the vehicle and taken her chances with the wildlife, rather than witness the murder of a magnificent creature.

The leopard jagged to the right and shot east into the rocky hills.

Rather than turn and follow, Mubanga kept driving north.

"Hey!" Klein yelled from the front of the vehicle. "The cat turned right!"

Mubanga completely ignored Klein and increased his speed.

The vehicle jolted so badly, Reese fought to keep from being thrown from her seat. The seat belt had long since frayed and broken. If she wanted to keep her teeth in her head, she had to brace herself on anything and everything to keep from launching through the window.

Klein flopped around like a rag doll on

the front of the vehicle, screaming for the driver to stop.

"Stop this vehicle!" Reese yelled over the roar of the engine. She reached for the handgun strapped to her thigh. Before she could pull it from its holster, Mubanga backhanded her in the face so hard, she saw stars.

Reese swayed, her fingers losing their grip on the door's armrest. A big jolt slammed her forward, and she banged her forehead against the dash. Pain sliced through her head, blinding her. Gray fog crept in around the edges of her vision. She fought to remain upright, retain consciousness and protect her client, but she felt herself slipping onto the floorboard of the Rover. One more bump, and she passed out.

A FEW MINUTES might have passed—or it could have been an hour, or even a day. Reese didn't know. All she knew was that the vehicle was still and Mubanga no longer sat behind the steering wheel. As her vision and clouded brain cleared, she pulled herself up to the seat, her hand going to the holster on her thigh, pain throbbing through her temple.

Her 9-millimeter Glock was gone.

The door jerked open at her side. Someone

grabbed her by her hair and yanked her out of her seat and onto the dirt.

She struggled to get her feet beneath her, but the man behind her swept out a leg, knocking her feet out from under her. Reese crumpled to the ground, her scalp screaming with the pain of being held steady by a handful of her hair.

"What the hell's going on?" she demanded. "Where's Mubanga?"

The men spoke in a language she didn't understand. The goon holding her by the hair kicked her in the side and shoved her away from him.

The relief on her scalp nearly brought tears to her eyes. At last, Reese was able to study her surroundings. Day had turned into dusk. Twenty dark-skinned men stood around her and Klein, each wielding a wicked-looking AK-47 rifle or a submachine gun. None looked like they were part of the Zambia Wildlife Authority. Their clothing was a mix of camouflage and rags. Mubanga was nowhere to be seen.

Ferrence lay unconscious on the ground, several feet away from her.

Some bodyguard she was. Her first international assignment, and her client was most likely dead. Her heart squeezed hard in her chest. Even though Ferrence had been a pain to work with, his father was nice and would be sad to lose his son. The man had paid a lot of money for her services to protect Ferrence, and she'd failed him. Reese hadn't wished ill on Ferrence. He was a job to her, but even more so, he was a human being. No one deserved to die on vacation in Zambia.

Since giving up mixed martial arts fighting, she'd put all her effort into her personal-protection-service start-up. She'd tapped on a few connections she'd gained while in the limelight of her fighting career and landed the job with the Kleins.

Ferrence hadn't wanted a bodyguard, thus, she'd come along at his father's insistence that the younger Klein needed an assistant to make his vacation in Zambia smooth and to his liking. Reese was also to pose as his assistant on his upcoming diplomatic visit to the Democratic Republic of the Congo.

Reese had stressed to both Ferrence and his father that she wasn't for hire for sexual favors. Not that Ferrence had listened to a word she'd said. She'd fought off more than one advance before the private jet had left the ground in New York, nearly crippling her client with a knee to the groin.

Since then, Ferrence had limited his advances to bumping into her whenever he could manage.

Now the spoiled son of a billionaire lay on the ground, still as death.

Reese inched toward him. In her peripheral vision, she kept an eye on the guns waving all around her. When she was only a foot away from Klein, the barrel of a rifle stopped her. She glanced up at her captor, a man with skin as black as the darkest night.

"I just want to see if he's still alive," she said.

"He alive," the man said in stilted English. "For now."

The sound of an engine drew her attention from her captor. That's when she noticed they were on the bank of a river. The motor noise came from a boat barreling toward them as though it would run aground before the driver slowed. Just as it neared the banks where the group of men stood, the driver pulled back on the throttle, and the craft slid to a gentle stop.

Two men reached for Klein, one grabbing his wrists, the other his ankles. They lifted him and slung him over the side of the boat, dropping him to the bottom.

The man beside Reese slipped the strap of his rifle over his shoulder and bent toward her.

Reese could easily take him, now that she was conscious and steadier on her feet. She could make a break for it, and might even make it to the tree line. She reasoned she could make a run for help. But that would mean abandoning the unconscious Klein. She was supposed to be protecting him, and she'd botched the job completely. Abandoning him now was not an option.

When the man reached for her arm, she jerked it away and rose to her feet. "I can walk."

His eyes narrowed, and he stared hard at her for a split second. Then he bent in half, hit her like a linebacker in her midsection and tossed her over his shoulder.

"Bastard!" she yelled. But she didn't fight hard. Her goal was to land in the boat next to Ferrence. When the time was right, and Ferrence was conscious, she'd find a way to escape. In the meantime, she let the man dump her into the boat, her body cushioned by Ferrence's limp form.

As the other men clambered aboard, Reese was able to check her charge for a pulse, which beat strongly. Reese breathed a sigh of relief. At least the man wasn't dead, and they were both tagged with GPS locator chips. She might yet repair the situation, if her captors didn't kill her first.

Three days later

DALTON SAMUEL LANDON, Diesel for short, leaned out of the open door of the MH-47 helicopter. Dusk wrapped around the helicopter, lengthening shadows between the trees and brush below and giving the team the concealment they needed to kick off Operation Silver Spoon.

While being lowered on cables, a Special Operations Craft-Riverine—or SOC-R boat—swayed over the muddy waters of the southern Congo River, before it was released and plopped into the water, rocking violently before it settled.

A bead of sweat dripped down Diesel's neck, into the collar of his shirt. Night swept over the sprawling marshlands of the Congo River in the southern province of the Democratic Republic of the Congo.

SEAL Boat Team 22 had been deployed to Djibouti, on the Horn of Africa, two days ago for this specific mission. They'd gone over the operation, studied the maps and gathered their equipment for what was now "showtime."

"The SOC-R's down!" Diesel shouted, his hand tightening on the rope, which was dangling from the helicopter to the boat below.

Wind from the rotors on each end of the chopper buffeted the craft and water below. One of the gunners hung out the door, searching for combatants, not expecting to find any this far south, but not willing to let his guard down.

"Ready?" Diesel yelled.

A shout rose up from the other members of SEAL Boat Team 22 inside the MH-47. With the helicopter hovering over the SOC-R, Diesel fast-roped from the helicopter and dropped into the boat. Once he had his balance, he took the helm and waited for the others to land.

The SOC-R's four-man crew consisted of one helmsman and three gunners. Two GAU-17/A machine guns mounted in the front of the boat, two side-mounted M240B light machine guns, one .50 caliber machine gun in the rear, two grenade launchers and sufficient ammo to take on a small army gave them enough firepower to withstand a limited war.

Hopefully, by traveling under the cover of night, they wouldn't have to use their supply of ammunition. They'd travel downriver using the GPS guidance system to the last known location of the rebels and their captives.

When all ten team members were on board, those who were designated took up positions behind each of the mounted weapons. The remaining SEALs had their M4A1 rifles with the SOPMOD upgrades in their hands, ready to take on any enemy threat.

Diesel handed the helm over to the helmsman and took up a position near the port bow. The helicopter lifted into the air and disappeared, heading south to await the call for extraction.

The helmsman opened up the throttle and sent the boat skimming through the marshlands of the headwaters of the Congo River.

The hostages had been taken three days ago. Their captors might be getting antsy and ready to kill them and cut their losses. Thus the need for speed, covering as much ground, or river, as possible that night. If all went well and they didn't get lost in the maze of tributaries, they might make it to the extraction location within a few hours.

Diesel and his team had been over and over the maps and satellite images provided by the Military intelligence gurus back in Langley, Virginia. Those were the guys who poured over hundreds of satellite images a day to locate threats or, in this situation, find the location of a kidnapped person being held for ransom. They sat behind their desks, staring at computer screens all day, and sometimes all night, long.

A shiver of revulsion slipped over Diesel. He'd rather shoot himself than man a desk inside an office all day long. Though extraction missions could be tricky and highly dangerous, he'd still rather face the danger than the boredom.

The military didn't always get involved in hostages being held for ransom. "We don't negotiate with terrorists" being the mantra repeated every time the hostage wasn't "worth" saving. But when the captive happened to be the Secretary of Defense's son, strings got pulled and men deployed.

Ferrence Klein, of the Manhattan Kleins, and the son of the Secretary of Defense,

Matthew Klein, had been taken hostage by a Congolese rebel faction and was being held for ransom, along with his bodyguard, Reese Brantley.

The official story out of Africa indicated Klein had been on a wild-game hunt and had gotten ahead of his guides, on the other side of the border, in Zambia.

Their vehicle had been set upon by Congolese rebels. Once the SUV had come to a halt, the driver ran away, and the rebels took Klein and Brantley into custody. Some of the witnesses claimed the driver was paid to bring the vehicle to the rebels and was allowed to go free once the deed was done.

A video message was broadcast on the Al Jazeera television network with Ferrence blubbering about paying the ransom or whatever it took to get him out of the jungle and back home to his beloved Manhattan. He didn't mention his bodyguard. The team could only assume Brantley was still alive, so they planned on bringing back two civilians.

Using the GPS, the helmsman navigated the river, speeding along as fast as he could in the growing darkness, skimming past what appeared to be drifting logs in the murky water. Those logs turned out to be crocodiles, floating on the surface. As the SOC-R neared, the crocs dove deep into the dark river, leaving no indication they'd been there other than a gentle rippling wave.

A chill slithered across the back of Diesel's neck. He did *not* want to fall into the water. He'd rather face a dozen Congolese rebels with only a knife than an African crocodile and its mouth full of razor-sharp teeth.

He spent the next couple hours on alert, watching the shoreline for any sign of movement or guards. They passed several villages on the banks with docks jutting out into the water. Unlike back in the States, these little towns were completely dark. Not a single light shining, now that the sun had set. Many didn't have electricity. Those who did conserved the energy, not seeing a need to light the darkness. Dark was meant for sleeping.

Diesel imagined the boat that had taken the two hostages upriver had passed much the same—unchallenged and in the dark, without raising suspicion or providing clues as to its destination.

Time passed slowly. Like a good SEAL, Diesel rested, conserving his strength for the task ahead. If they didn't run into any trouble, they'd arrive well before midnight. That's when the fun would begin.

What seemed like a lifetime later, the helmsman called out, "Twenty minutes to LZ."

Diesel's pulse ratcheted up several notches, and his hand tightened on the M4A1 rifle in his hand. With only twenty minutes until they reached their landing zone, they could potentially run into Congolese rebels soon.

Ten minutes passed, and the helmsman slowed the boat to a crawl, hugging the starboard banks, using the shadows cast by the moonlight as concealment, while he searched for a good spot to tie off. Those who weren't staying with the boat would cover the rest of the distance on foot. That was seven of the ten-man team. They'd push through the trees and bushes of the now jungle terrain to their destination, where the green blips on the GPS location device led them.

A break in the overhanging limbs led to a narrow tributary, just wide enough to wedge the SOC-R into and allow the landing party to disembark.

Before he led the team off the boat, Diesel slipped his night vision goggles into position over his eyes. He scanned the shoreline, searching for any green heat signatures, whether they be man or beast. Life along the Congo River was rife with crocodiles, and if that wasn't dangerous enough, they were getting close to an area known for their bands of gorillas. Now wasn't the time to be wrestling crocs or gorillas. They had a job to do.

Nothing moved, and no green lights glowed in his night vision goggles. Diesel hopped over the side of the boat and landed on the soft, muddy slope of the riverbank. He scrambled up to a drier purchase and provided cover for the others as they disembarked. The SOC-R would remain hidden until the team returned with the hostages. Helicopter backup was a last resort.

Operation Silver Spoon was a covert operation. The Congolese Government wasn't to know the US Navy had sent people uninvited into their country. If members of the team were captured, they were to escape at any cost or disavow their connection to the US Navy and US Government. Though their weapons and equipment were dead giveaways, they each wore solid-black clothing without rank or insignia of any kind, and they didn't carry any identification cards or tags.

Each man knew the risks. He also knew

his fellow SEALs wouldn't leave a single man behind—not for long, at least.

As the last man climbed out of the SOC-R, Diesel moved out, following the river, moving several yards in from the shore. He slid from shadow to shadow, carefully scanning the path ahead. He ran quickly and as quietly as possible. Stealth was their friend. If they could get into the camp, subdue the rebels and get out without stirring up a firestorm, they would make it back to Zambia by morning, and Djibouti by lunchtime.

Diesel shook his head. As much as they went through possible scenarios, or practiced different approaches, nothing ever quite turned out like they planned. Sometimes the weather played a role in gumming up the works. Sometimes the tangos they were going up against were a little more sophisticated or armed than they'd anticipated. And sometimes fate dealt them a crappy hand. Bottom line: they had to be ready to roll with the punches.

Diesel spied the first tango fifteen minutes from their LZ. "Tango at ten o'clock, twenty meters." He held up his fist and lowered himself to a squatting position, studying the guard posted near the riverbank.

After a couple minutes of observation, Diesel determined the guard was lying in a prone position without moving. He was either dead or asleep at his post.

Either way, Diesel had to insure he wouldn't raise the alarm.

"I'll take him," Diesel said. "Buck, cover me."

Graham Buckner, or Buck for short, moved up to take Diesel's position. Though he was the team corpsman, or medic, he was an excellent sharpshooter. He knelt on one knee and propped his elbow, staring down the scope fixed to the barrel of his M4A1 rifle. "Got your six. Go."

Diesel shifted his night vision goggles up onto his helmet, slipped his rifle strap over his shoulder, pulled his KA-BAR knife from the scabbard on his ankle and circled wide, coming in behind his prey, who faced the river.

The man woke at the exact moment Diesel pressed the blade to his throat. He didn't have time to shout or even whisper a cry before Diesel dispatched the man.

Slipping his night vision goggles back in place, Diesel studied the area to his north. A small camp had been set up with makeshift tents. Several men leaned against trees, their rifles resting in their laps. By the way the men's heads were drooped to the side, Diesel could tell they were fast asleep. The faint glow of heat indicated two warm bodies in the nearest tent, one in the next closest tent and three more in the farthest tent. One man stood in front of the tent with two people inside. It had to be the tent containing the hostages. The one man stood guard, while all the others slept.

Unfortunately, that one man could easily wake the others, and then all hell would break loose.

"I count eleven tangos, but I can't see the back side of the camp," Diesel whispered into his mic. "Buck, bound to my position. Harm, cover. Pitbull, Big Jake and T-Mac, swing wide and head north to cover the flank."

Each man gave a quiet affirmative and proceeded to spread out.

Once Buck took Diesel's position, Diesel motioned Harm forward. Together, they approached the camp, easing toward the one guard on duty, his rifle held loosely in his hands.

"Cover me," Diesel said.

Harm nodded. He had a silencer on his

M4A1. He could drop the man in a heart-beat should trouble erupt. In the meantime, Diesel needed to get to the tent with the two hostages, take out the guard and spirit the hostages away before the rest of the camp got wind of their little operation.

Chapter Two

Reese didn't have much of an opportunity to escape. Their captors had seen fit to leave one of their members in the tent with her and Klein. Not only that, but they'd tied her hands behind her back and bound her ankles. They'd done the same to Ferrence. When he'd surfaced from unconsciousness, he'd been angry and scared. The captors only had to threaten pain and torture to get Ferrence to beg on video for the ransom money they wanted. One of the men had recorded his plea on a cell phone and left to take the video somewhere he could get cell tower reception.

They claimed to be Congolese rebels fighting for the freedom of their country to decide how to be governed, but Reese doubted they were fighting for anyone but themselves. Their leader was a big, bulky black man with a scar on the side of his face. He wore bandoliers filled with bullets, crisscrossing his chest like armor, and carried a submachine gun, waving it at anyone who angered him. His men had called him something that sounded like Bosco Mutombo.

Once their captors had their video of Ferrence's plea, he and Reese had been left confined to the tent, allowed to go out only to relieve themselves under the watchful eyes of armed men.

Reese had been sized up and threatened with sexual abuse, but left alone when she said they would more likely get their money if both she and Ferrence were not harmed. Otherwise, they'd send in the US Army, Navy, Air Force and Marines to blow them off the face of the earth.

One man translated for the others, and they all laughed, though the laughter had a certain nervous edge to it.

Reese didn't care, as long as they didn't touch her.

A moan sounded from her client's direction.

Inching her way across the bare ground, Reese moved toward Ferrence, careful not to draw the attention of the guard sitting with his back to her. He glanced toward her every two or three minutes, but otherwise, didn't seem concerned that she might find a way to escape. He had an old video gaming device in his hand and seemed more interested in his game score than his captives.

The guard's head came up, and he glanced toward her.

Reese closed her eyes and let her head slump forward like she'd just nodded off.

Through her lashes, she could see the man's eyes narrow. He looked back at his video game. The light blinked out on it, and he shook it, muttering beneath his breath.

Reese almost laughed. She suspected the battery had died. Since she hadn't heard a generator, and there weren't any other lights on in the camp that she could see through the canvas of the tent, the guard wouldn't be playing his game for the rest of his time there with no way to recharge the battery.

The man stood, ducked his head and stepped out of the tent.

Finally alone in the tent, Reese scooted on her butt toward Ferrence and whispered into his ear. "Wake up."

He moaned, rolled onto his back and frowned when he couldn't move his hands.

For a moment, he lay still. Then he asked, "Any news?"

She shook her head, and then realized he wouldn't see the movement in the dark. "None. We can't wait to be rescued. We need to get ourselves out of this mess."

"And hide in a jungle full of snakes, gorillas and who the hell knows what else?" He shook his head. "No way. I'll wait for my father to pay the ransom and be escorted out of here in one of his helicopters."

She snorted. "Wake up and smell the coffee, Ferrence." As soon as she mentioned coffee, her belly rumbled. The only thing they'd been given to eat were a couple of bananas and unbaked sweet potatoes. Fortunately, they'd been supplied bottled water to drink, thus saving their stomachs from parasites. But the last bottle of water had been on the second morning. "It's been three days. If they don't get their ransom money soon, they might decide to kill us and hide the bodies."

"We're still equipped with the GPS tracking devices," Ferrence argued. "They're probably on their way as we speak."

"Are you willing to risk it? Do you really think these men will wait much longer? Just today, they were fighting among themselves.

At least sit up and let me see if I can untie the ropes on your wrists."

He did as she asked, scooting around to put his back to hers.

Reese had already tried to untie her bonds or to rub the rope against something coarse, but she was confined to the tent, and nothing inside the tent presented itself as a coarse surface.

She fumbled with the ropes on Ferrence's wrists, finally finding the end and working it back through one of the knots.

She'd broken out in a sweat by the time she'd freed Ferrence's hands. "Now me. Untie my hands."

"When I get my feet done." He leaned away from her and grunted.

Reese grit her teeth. "Think about it, Ferrence. If you untie my wrists first, we can both untie our feet at the same time."

"I've got it," he said, triumphantly, and then turned to work at the knots on her wrists. "Yours are tighter." He blew out a frustrated breath. "I don't think I can get it."

"Try harder," she urged.

Finally, she felt the ropes give, and she shook her hands free. She immediately bent to the task of untying her legs. "If the guard comes back, pretend your wrists and ankles are still tied."

"Like hell. I'm getting out of here."

"Wait until I'm free," she said. "We need to stick together."

"You're fast. You can catch up." He lifted the back of the tent, stared out at the night and whispered, "I don't see anyone out there. I think we can make a run for it."

"Wait—" Her hands still fumbling with the knots around her ankles, Reese couldn't lunge after Ferrence. He was out the back of the tent and gone.

"Son of a b—" The end slipped through the knot and the ropes fell away from her ankles. A grunt sounded outside the front of the tent, and something fell, landing hard against the ground.

Not willing to stick around to find out what it was, Reese ducked beneath the bottom of the tent, rolled out and sprang to her feet. She ran for the nearest trees and bushes.

A shout rang out to her right, and then all hell broke loose.

Shots were fired, men yelled and chaos reigned. Reese didn't slow down, didn't stop, just kept running until she hit a wall. She hit the obstacle so hard, she bounced off and landed on her butt. Refusing to be captured again, she shot to her feet and dodged to the left.

A hand snaked out and grabbed her arm.

She rolled beneath the arm, sank her elbow into what she hoped was the man's belly and hit what felt like solid steel. Pain shot through her arm. She'd likely chipped her elbow.

Whoever had hold of her was wearing an armored plate. Having been caught and tortured before, she refused to be a victim again. She kicked her foot hard, connecting with the man's shin.

He yelled and almost lost his grip on her arm.

Reese took advantage of the loosened hold and yanked herself free.

Before she could run two steps, arms wrapped around her waist from behind, and she was lifted off the ground. She struggled, kicked and wiggled, but nothing she could do would free her of the man holding her.

"Damn it, hold still," a man's voice whispered against her ear, his breath warm and surprisingly minty.

Reese recognized the American accent immediately. "Who are you? Why are you holding me captive?" She fought again. Many

Americans hired out as mercenaries. This could be one of them.

"I'm not here to hurt you." He grunted when her heel made contact with his thigh. "Damn it, I'm here to rescue you." He dropped her to the ground so fast, she lost her footing and crumpled into a heap at his feet.

More gunfire sounded behind her. Where the hell was Ferrence? Had the rebels shot him for trying to escape?

This time, when she tried to get up, the man in the armored vest laid a hand on her shoulder and dropped low beside her. "Stay down. You don't know the direction they're shooting." He stayed close to her, and then he said. "Get him out of here."

"What?" she asked.

"We're getting Klein out of here."

"Not without me," she said. "He's my client." Reese started to get up, but that hand on her shoulder kept her down. "Who are you?"

"My team was sent to get you two out of here."

"Your team?" She glanced around. "Are you Spec Ops?"

"Shh," he said. "Someone's coming."

In the limited light making its way through the canopy of foliage, Reese could make out the silhouette of a man carrying a weapon. She lay low against the ground. The man beside her flattened himself, as well.

Neither moved a muscle as the man carrying what appeared to be an AK-47 passed inches away from where they lay.

More shouts rose up from the rebels in the camp. A motor sounded close by, and flashlights lit up the area.

The man with the AK-47 turned and almost walked over them on his way back to camp. Thankfully, he must have been too blinded by the lights to see what was right next to him.

Once the rebel fighter was out of hearing range, the man beside Reese spoke softly. "Looks like they're getting into their boat."

Reese peered through the darkness. All she could see were flashlights heading away from her and the occasional man caught in the beam. The camp was emptying out, heading for the river.

"They're heading south," the man said softly. "Your direction. Don't wait on me. Get Klein out of here, now. I have Brantley. We'll find our own way back. I'll contact you when we're out of danger. Don't argue. Just go."

Reese was only half-listening to her rescuer's side of a conversation. Some of the men appeared to be climbing aboard a boat. The others turned around, shining lights toward the jungle. She tugged on the sleeve of the man beside her. "We've got a problem." She rose onto her haunches. "Some of them are coming this way with flashlights."

BRANTLEY WAS RIGHT. Diesel glanced around. The men were coming toward them and spreading out, heading south along the river. A shout went up when they found their sentry.

"Follow me. And for the love of God, stay low," he commanded. He led the way deeper into the jungle and turned north, praying he didn't get them lost. He figured, as long as he had a GPS device on his wrist, he'd be all right. If they had to, they'd travel all the way to Kinshasa, the capital of the Democratic Republic of the Congo, and show up on the doorstep of the US Embassy, claiming some lame excuse of being tourists who'd fallen off a riverboat cruise.

In the meantime, they had to get away from the gun-toting rebels who'd just as soon shoot first and ask questions of a corpse later.

Especially since they'd found one of their own dead.

A shout sounded behind him. He glanced back at Brantley. Lights flashed toward them. "Run," he urged.

They gave up all attempt at quiet and charged through the jungle. The head start they had on the rebels would help, but they couldn't keep running forever. They needed to find a place to hide.

His lungs already burning, the heat dragging him down, Diesel could imagine the woman behind him had to be dying by now. He reached back, captured Brantley's hand and pulled her along with him. When they arrived at a stand of huge trees with low-hanging limbs, Diesel aimed for them, slowing as he neared.

"Why are we slowing down? They'll catch up to us," Brantley said between ragged breaths.

Diesel cupped his hands. "Climb."

"No. Wait." The woman ripped her shirt and ran away from him.

"Where the hell are you going?" he called out to her in a whisper he hoped couldn't be heard by their pursuers.

In the pale glow from what little starlight

penetrated the canopy, Brantley raced to the far edge of the clearing that surrounded the base of the tree and hung the piece of fabric on a bush. As quickly as she'd left, she returned to where Diesel again bent and held out his cupped hands. If they didn't hurry, that little bit of fabric hanging on a bush wouldn't make a difference.

"Go!" he urged.

Still, she hesitated. "I don't know."

"Don't think. Just climb."

Shouts in the jungle behind them had her stepping into the palms of his hands. He boosted her up to the first limb. When she had her balance, he handed her his rifle, and then pulled himself up beside her.

Without waiting for him to instruct her, Brantley climbed from limb to limb, rising high up the trunk to the vegetation that would provide sufficient concealment from the men wielding flashlights and weapons below.

As the men neared the tree, Brantley came to a stop. Diesel followed suit. For the next fifteen minutes, they sat silent in the tree.

Diesel breathed, held his breath and listened.

The sound of footsteps below indicated the

men had reached the base of the tree. A light shined up into the branches.

Diesel glanced up.

Brantley hugged the trunk, pressing her body against the hard wood, making herself appear to be as much a part of the tree as its bark.

Diesel had laid his rifle along a thick horizontal branch, and then he laid himself across the branch, as well, bringing his feet up behind him to keep them from dangling over the sides. If he slipped an inch to the left or the right, he might fall off the branch and all the way to the ground. He didn't think about falling. Instead, he focused on his balance and maintaining his silence.

A man below yelled. The flashlights were turned away from the branches of the tree and shined toward the far side of the clearing. Footsteps pounded through the brush, toward the jungle and way from the two people up in the tree.

Soon, the sound of humans faded away, and the creatures of the night sent up their own song.

"They're gone," Reese said. "Should we get down?"

Diesel sat up, his legs straddling the big

branch. When he scooted back into the trunk, he found that there was enough room for two people to sit comfortably without falling out of the tree. "We're staying the night here."

"You've got to be kidding," she said.

"I'm not sure which direction the rebels went. If we get down and follow them, they might decide to turn around and head back to camp. If we turn back the way we came, we might run into whoever they left behind."

"Yeah, yeah. I get it. If we go deeper into the jungle, we might be lost for good, and the river is full of its own dangers." She sighed. "I guess being up a tree for the night beats getting shot at or eaten by crocodiles…" Her words trailed off.

Diesel chuckled. "You don't sound very enthusiastic."

"I might be if I wasn't just a little petrified of heights." Her voice shook, and her teeth chattered.

"You're kidding, right?" Diesel shined his flashlight with the red filtered lens up at her.

She remained glued to the tree above him, even though the enemy threat had moved on. As the light touched her face, she opened her eyes and looked down. "Oh, hell." She squeezed them shut. "Shouldn't have done that. No, no, no. Shouldn't have done that."

"What? Shined the light up at you?"

"No," she said, her teeth clattering together so hard that Diesel was afraid she'd chip one.

"No. I shouldn't have looked down." Brantley's arms tightened around the tree. "Now that I'm up here, I might as well stay awhile. I certainly won't be getting down anytime soon."

Good grief, the woman was beyond terrified. "Don't move," Diesel said. "I'm coming up."

"Don't move, he says." Brantley laughed, the sound without amusement. "Trust me when I say, I couldn't let go if I wanted to. So much for all the MMA training. It doesn't help you conquer all of your fears. No, you have to climb up to the top of a giant tree to test the theory. You couldn't just stand on the edge of a cliff. Noooo. You had to climb up a really tall tree in the dark, in a jungle, with an absolute stranger who could be just as much the enemy as the people who kidnapped you."

A smile twitched at the corners of Diesel's mouth at Brantley's long monologue. He knew she was talking to keep from freaking out, but it was funny and kind of cute. She'd kept up with him in their mad dash to evade her captors. And she was a bodyguard and appeared to be capable of protecting herself. To Diesel, that spelled one tough chick.

Until she'd climbed a tree and looked down toward the ground.

Diesel pulled himself up to the next branch and the next, until he finally slung his leg over the limb Brantley was straddling, hugging the trunk with all of her might.

Diesel scooted closer.

Brantley glanced over her shoulder, nervously. "Don't knock me off."

"Wasn't going to." He inched toward her. "You know, there's enough room for two to sit here all night."

"So you say." She didn't let go of the tree trunk.

In the dark, Diesel couldn't see her fingertips, but could imagine them curled into the bark.

When he was close enough to touch her back, she flinched.

"I'm not going to knock you off. I was hoping to reassure you that this limb is big enough for the two of us." He wrapped his body around hers. "You're as tense as a tightly wound rattlesnake with a brand new button on his tail."

Brantley snorted. "Did you just fall off a horse in Texas?"

Diesel chuckled. "How did you know I was from Texas?"

"Lucky guess." She inhaled, her back rubbing against Diesel's chest. Letting the breath out in a long stream, she laughed. "I don't suppose you know of anyone who'd hire a bodyguard who couldn't keep her client safe?"

"Not off the top of my head. But then the odds were stacked against you on this assignment, from what I know."

"Damned guide was in on the kidnapping," she stated. "I should have seen it. Hell, I should have shot him when I realized he was taking us the wrong way." She shook her head. "But I didn't."

"You might have had an international incident on your hands had you killed him."

"Yeah, and he was driving when I considered it, at a breakneck speed, with Klein out front on the hood."

"On the hood?"

"You know, in some kind of seat they rig

up for the hunter. He was going after a leop-ard."

"I thought they were protected."

"Ferrence paid a hefty price for a real sa-fari hunt. I think the guide assured him he could shoot just about anything." The disgust in her voice was evident.

"You don't much care for Mr. Klein?"

"Not really, but that doesn't mean I wish ill on him."

"Then why work for him?"

"I'm not. I work—*worked*—for his father, Matthew Klein. He hired me to protect his son. And a lot of good that did. I wouldn't be surprised if he demands a refund."

"Don't be so hard on yourself."

"Why not? I didn't do my job." She snorted. "I can't even get down out of this tree."

"We'll worry about that in the morning, when we can see what we're doing."

"Hell, I'm putting my trust in a stranger. I don't even know you."

"We can fix that. Hi. I'm Dalton Samuel Landon, but my friends call me Diesel." He reached around her, peeled her hand off the tree and gave it an awkward shake. "And you are?" As soon as she let go, her hand found its way back to the tree.

"You must already know who I am since you were sent to rescue us."

"Reese Brantley," he supplied. "How did a girl like you end up as a bodyguard to Ferrence Klein?"

She stiffened. "What do you mean *a girl like you*?"

He chuckled. "Sorry. I meant how did you get stuck as a bodyguard to the Klein legacy?"

Her body remained rigid for a few seconds longer, and then she relaxed. "His father didn't want him to know he'd hired a bodyguard. He told Ferrence I would be his assistant while he was in Africa. Had he hired a male, Ferrence would have guessed."

Diesel nodded. "And Ferrence didn't want daddy's protection?"

"No. Not when he'd made plans to hunt endangered species." Again, Reese's body tensed. "Had I known he'd come to hunt anything but some plentiful deer, I'd have told his father where his son could go."

"I take it he was more interested in a trophy than food?"

"He was hunting a leopard when the driver veered off course." She half-turned toward him. "By the way, where are we? I have a feeling we aren't in Zambia anymore."

Diesel's arms tightened around her. "We're not. We're in the Democratic Republic of the Congo."

The woman sat stiff. "Okay. Well. We'll just have to get the hell out of here. I don't suppose your team is coming back anytime soon?"

"They will." He couldn't say when. Since they had Klein to get out, the powers that pulled the strings might not want to redeploy the team to extract one SEAL and one civilian. Not in a hostile country. And not when they weren't supposed to be there to begin with. With current tensions between the new presidential administration and international trade relations, Diesel wasn't sure they'd risk a second insertion into the DRC.

"In the meantime," Reese said, "we'll have to get out of this area, or risk being caught."

A sound alerted Diesel. He touched Reese's arm. "Shh," he said softly. "I hear someone coming."

Chapter Three

Reese froze and listened. The animals and insects were suddenly silent. A slight breeze rustled the leaves around her. Then the snap of a twig alerted her to movement below.

Someone whispered in a language she barely recognized, and didn't understand. Then shots rang out, and the rapid report of a semiautomatic weapon filled the air.

Diesel pressed his body against her, smashing her against the tree trunk. Something hit close to where her fingers dug into the bark, splintering wood fragments over her hand.

As quickly as the burst of bullets began, they ended. Voices below spoke in rapid-fire anger. Then they moved away, heading back toward the camp where Reese and Ferrence had been held hostage for several days. As much as she hated being high up in a tree, she'd rather face the heights than her former captors.

Diesel remained pressed to her back for a couple minutes after the sounds of movement below had dissipated.

The solid strength of his body was unexpectedly reassuring. Reese frowned. She didn't like that she needed reassurance. Having spent the last three years rebuilding her life and confidence, she didn't need a man to reassure her about anything. She was the bodyguard, not Diesel.

Then again, she'd failed in her first real assignment as a bodyguard and had fallen into a situation she'd sworn she'd never allow herself to be in, ever again. She'd been captured. This time, her captors hadn't been as quick to torture and rape her. Had they tried, she'd have died fighting them off. Never again would she allow anyone to violate her, to abuse her like she'd been abused at the hands of the Taliban in Afghanistan.

The mere thought of what they'd done to her had the usual effect on her. She broke out in a cold sweat, her heart raced and she felt as if she might explode if she didn't get away and suck more air into her lungs.

"I can't breathe," she whispered through tight lips.

Immediately, the man behind her eased back. "Were you hit?"

"No," she said and dragged air into her lungs. The desire to move, to get away, took hold of her and refused to let go. At that moment, she had the uncontrollable urge to throw herself out of the tree. But she couldn't. The enemy could return. They might be lying in wait just beyond the clearing around the tree, hoping to capture them as they came out of hiding.

Instead, she bit down hard on her lip, clenched her fists and started counting to one hundred. Her body shook with the effort to control her reaction.

"Are you sure you weren't hit?" Diesel asked, his voice quiet, his mouth close to her ear, his body leaning into hers.

Reese couldn't respond, couldn't utter a word. She remained focused on not losing her cool.

Diesel's hands gripped her arms and pulled her back against his chest. "You're shaking like a paint mixer. It's okay. They're gone," he said, holding her close.

"I'm okay," Reese said, forcing the words out from between her teeth.

Diesel's arms wrapped around her midsection and held on tightly. "Clearly, you aren't."

"You don't have to hold me," she insisted, hating herself for her reaction and the need to feel his arms around her. "I can manage on my own."

"I'm afraid to let go. You might shake yourself right out of this tree."

"I'll manage," she insisted. "Please. Let go."

When he moved his arms away from her, Reese let go of the tree long enough to hug herself to ward off the chills threatening to take over. When she touched her arm where his hand had been, she felt something warm, wet and sticky. Blood? She felt around, but nothing hurt.

Because the blood wasn't hers.

"Hey." She half turned. "Were you hit?"

"I got nicked. But it's just a flesh wound. I'm fine," he said. "I'm more worried about getting us out of here and away from our friends with the AK-47s."

"You should let me look at your wound."

"It's not like you can see in the dark, and

I'm not willing to risk turning on a flashlight for a little scrape."

Reese would bet her best pair of hiking boots the wound was more than a mere scrape. "At least let me apply a pressure bandage to stop the bleeding. Where is it?"

"It's okay," he said, his tone sharp.

"Look, you dripped blood on to my arm. If you're still dripping, you might leave a trail for the goons to follow." She grabbed the hem of her shirt and, carefully and as quietly as possible, ripped off a section. She tried to turn on the tree limb and nearly tipped over the side. Her heart clattered against the walls of her chest.

Diesel held on to her arm to steady her. "Wait until we get down from here."

"For all we know, we'll be up here for a while." She shook her head. "Let me feel for myself. Where is it?" She touched his wrist and moved up his arm.

"Higher," he said.

Reese ran her hand up his thick, solid forearm to the bicep. When her fingers encountered fresh, warm blood, she knew she'd found the source of the leak. "It's more than a scrape. You might need stitches."

"I don't. But if it makes you feel better, you

can wrap it up to keep me from bleeding and leaving a trail."

"Damn right I will." Pushing her fear of heights to the side, she maneuvered herself around to face him, her knees touching his, making it hard for her to reach his arm. She bent close, but still couldn't get to the spot she needed to reach. "Could you lean closer?" she asked.

"Oh, for Pete's sake." He grabbed her hips, lifted her off the tree limb and deposited her onto his lap, her legs straddling his hips.

Heat rushed into Reese's cheeks and farther south to her core. She'd never sat in a man's lap quite like this before. The angle of their contact was more than intimate, and completely befuddled her thinking. Thankfully, it also took her mind off the fact they were over twenty-five feet in the air, perched on a tree limb.

With his arms holding her firmly around her waist, she went to work wrapping the fabric around his injured arm. The fact he could move it as well as he did was proof it wasn't as bad as she'd thought. But any injury in the jungle and subsequent blood loss could be life-threatening, especially if it became infected. She did the best she could in the dark. The sooner they got her rescuer to a health-care facility, the better.

"That's as good as I can manage, without seeing the actual wound," Reese said. "You can let go, now."

"And if I don't want to?" he said, his voice rich and thick like smooth heated chocolate, spreading into every pore of her skin.

Reese's breath lodged in her lungs, and a thrill rippled through her, culminating at the point where her bottom rested on his thighs. Good Lord. She could *not* be having lusty thoughts about a complete stranger, while facing one of her most irrational fears in the canopy of a jungle tree.

Diesel's arms tightened around her for a moment and then loosened. "I'll balance you, while you turn around." He grabbed her around her waist and eased her backward.

Reese rested a hand on his broad shoulder, until she was forced to release it and turn to clutch at the tree's trunk.

A second later, Diesel moved from behind her and dropped to the limb below. Once again, he wrapped his strong hands around her waist. "When I lift you, wrap your arms around my neck and slide your body down mine. Your feet will land on another limb."

"C-can't we wait until morning?"

"The more I consider it, the more I'm afraid that if we wait until morning, the men in the camp will see us. We need to get as far from them as possible tonight."

Reese knew what Diesel said was valid, but climbing down from a tree was so much more frightening than going up. The warmth of his hands gripping her waist gave her the courage to let go of the tree trunk and transfer her hold to his neck. She wrapped her arms around him so tightly, she was sure she practically strangled him.

He settled her feet onto the limb in front of him and urged her to ease up on the stranglehold around his neck. Once he had her sitting on the lower branch, he leaned close. "See? Not so bad."

"Easy for you to say," she grumbled. But it wasn't so bad. She still couldn't see the ground, and maybe that was a blessing.

"I'm going all the way to the ground," he whispered into her ear, his warm breath stirring the loose hairs against her cheek. "Don't move a muscle, until I return with the all clear."

She nodded, wanting to tell him to be careful, but knowing it was a wasted sentiment.

The man was obviously trained in tactics and evasion. He knew how to steal through the night like a shadow.

He slipped away before she could change her mind or cling to him and beg him to stay. While Diesel was gone, she counted her breaths, praying he didn't walk into a trap and get himself killed.

He was gone for what felt like an eternity. When she'd about given up hope of his return and started to consider her own descent from the tree, she heard the soft rustle of fabric and a gentle grunt. Diesel pulled himself up to the limb below her, his head on level with her thigh. All she could see was his black silhouette against the dark backdrop of the jungle and the pale whites of his eyes.

"Miss me?" he asked.

She snorted. "Hardly," she lied. "What took you so long?"

"I went back to the camp. The men there had settled in for the night. The ones that took off on the boat hadn't returned."

"God, I hope they didn't catch up to the rest of your team." She prayed Ferrence made it back to civilization without further incident. Then, at the very least, she wouldn't be responsible for his death.

"Don't worry. There are enough of them to take on anything those rebels have in store. It's you and me I'm worried about."

"Any ideas?"

"We head north, following the river. Hopefully, we will run across someone who can help get us to safety. But first, we have to get you out of this tree."

"I can do it by myself," she said with a lot more confidence than she felt.

"Okay then. It's tricky in the dark. If you need to hold on to me, I'll be here."

Taking a deep breath, Reese leaned on to her belly and dropped both legs over the side of the limb she'd been sitting on.

A hand on her bottom steadied her and helped guide her to the branch below. Once she had her feet firmly on the thick limb, she dropped to a sitting position. Using this method, she slowly eased herself to the lowest limb.

Diesel dropped to the earth and touched her thigh. "Swing your other leg over and drop. I'll catch you."

"I'm a full-grown woman, not a small child. If I throw myself out of this tree, I could hurt both of us. Besides, you're injured."

"Do you always argue this much? If we don't hurry, those goons will be on top of us. Now do as I said," he commanded.

Reese closed her eyes, swung her leg over the limb and slid out of the tree.

True to his word, Diesel caught her. Granted, he staggered backward several steps until he got his feet under him. Still, he held her in his arms.

"You can put me down," she said. "I can stand on my own feet." She touched his arm where she'd tied the cloth around his wound. It was soaked with blood. "Damn it, Diesel, you're still bleeding."

He let her feet drop down, and she slid down his muscular front, feeling every line, ripple and indentation as she went. By the time her feet touched the ground, her body was on fire. What was it about this man that awakened in her something she thought died back in Afghanistan?

Reese quickly stepped away, her breathing ragged, her thoughts flustered. She was glad for the darkness, as she figured it would hide how red her cheeks must be. "We need to get you to a doctor. You might need stitches and antibiotics."

"I'll live. I won't need any of that if we

don't get out of here ASAP." He grabbed her hand and took off, running north of the camp.

Reese ran with him, doing her best not to trip over branches and fall flat on her face. They didn't have time for broken legs. The few shafts of starlight making it through the canopy were all she had to light her way. She prayed they didn't run into any crocodiles or gorillas in the darkness.

DIESEL KEPT UP a grueling pace, determined to get as far away from the camp of Congolese rebels as he could before daring to slow down.

To Reese's credit, she did a good job keeping up with him. Based on the brief moments he'd held her in his arms, he could tell she didn't have a spare ounce of flesh on her. Her body was honed, her muscles tight and well-defined.

Eventually, they slowed and moved at a fast walk, following the river, keeping it within twenty or thirty yards—close enough to maintain their bearings, but hopefully not too close they would run into a crocodile lazing on the bank. The river twisted in undulating curls, making it hard to follow exactly. Despite the meandering nature of the waterway, Diesel felt confident they were still within fairly easy reach of the water.

If only they could come across some sort of civilization—someone who had a telephone would be great. The river had villages along the way, but Diesel had no idea of how far it was between each. They couldn't remain on the run for long. And as soon as they stopped, the mosquitos would eat them alive and spread who knew what kind of diseases. Fortunately, he'd packed a lightweight mosquito net in one of his cargo pockets. As soon as he felt they'd gotten far enough away from the rebels, he'd find another tree big enough for both of them to sleep in.

They'd been fortunate thus far that they hadn't run into any other wildlife. That luck couldn't last forever. Big cats, gorillas, hippos and crocodiles were just a few of the dangers that lurked along the banks of the Congo. The two-legged creatures could be every bit as treacherous.

After they'd been on the move for two hours, Diesel could feel his energy waning. The wound on his arm hadn't stopped bleeding and had begun to throb. They needed to stop and rest soon.

He came across a clearing in the jungle,

where the trees on the edges were large enough to provide shelter for them.

When he stopped beside one of the trees, he turned to Reese.

"Please tell me you're just stopping to catch your breath," she said, bending over to rest her hands on her knees, her breathing labored. "You know how I am about heights. It's not something I'll ever outgrow."

"It's the safest place to sleep. If you want to stay on the ground, you're welcome to it. You might be sharing it with snakes, big cats, warthogs and gorillas. The mosquitoes alone might kill you. I'm going up. And I have a mosquito net."

Reese straightened and slapped at her cheek. "Mosquito net? What armed aggressor carries a mosquito net into an operation?"

"One who's going into the jungle. I brought the very basics for survival, in case I was separated from my team."

"How fortuitous. I don't suppose you have a cell phone in one of your pockets?"

Diesel could see the pale outline of her face in the murky darkness, but not the expression in her eyes. "We were equipped with two-way radio headsets, but we're too far away from my team to communicate, and the chances of finding a cell phone transmission tower in the jungle are slim to none. The cell phone I have probably won't work until we make it all the way to Kinshasa."

Reese tipped up her head. "I really hate climbing trees," she muttered and grabbed a hold of a low-hanging branch. "And what will keep a big cat from climbing the tree with us?"

"I think we can fend off a big cat in a tree easier than we can on the ground. I do have a weapon."

"With that weapon, couldn't we fight off everything on the ground, then?" Reese pulled herself up onto the first branch.

"We need to get some rest. You might not like heights, but I'm not fond of snakes. I'd rather take my chances in a tree than on the ground."

"Fine. I'm climbing. But don't expect me to like it," she grumbled.

He chuckled and climbed up behind her. "I didn't expect you to." He handed her a tube. "Drink."

"Where did you get water?"

"I have a water container on my back. Standard issue. Beats the hell out of canteens."

She sipped and then sat back. "I didn't realize how thirsty I was. As humid as it is, you'd think we wouldn't need to drink."

"All the more reason to keep hydrated." He tucked the tube away and tipped his head up. "Wait here."

She raised her hand. "I'm not going anywhere."

Diesel climbed higher, found a fork in a sturdy branch, broke off some boughs full of leaves and twigs and laid them in the fork. He figured if the gorillas could make nests, he could too. Soon he had a relatively secure place for them to sleep through the remainder of the night. He hooked the mosquito netting from a branch above and camouflaged it with leaves.

When he was satisfied, he turned to climb back down, only to find Reese scooting out on the limb.

"I got tired of waiting," she said.

The meager light that found its way through the canopy gave just enough illumination for her to see what he'd been working on. "Looks like a cocoon."

"It is, in a way. Crawl on in."

"You sure it'll hold me?" she asked, still hesitating.

"I've been all over it. It's pretty sturdy."

Reese eased beneath the netting and stopped. "Can we be seen from below?"

"Won't know until daylight. Go ahead. Get some rest. I'll take first watch."

"No way. You're the injured party. I should have been up here doing all this while you rested."

"I'm fine. It's just a—"

"Flesh wound," she finished. "You men. You could have a sucking chest wound and you'd still call it a flesh wound. At least let me do a better job on the bandage, now that we're far enough away from our pursuers."

"If it'll get you inside, okay." He slipped into the nest beside her and turned his arm toward her.

"Got a flashlight? I'd like to see what I'm working with."

He handed her a small flashlight with a red lens. "Better than nothing and not as visible from a distance."

She nodded, wedged the flashlight into the netting and pointed it at Diesel's arm. Then she tried to untie the knotted bloody fabric.

Every time her knuckles grazed the wound, Diesel flinched.

"It's getting red and puffy around the wound. You need medical attention."

"Why? I have you." He winked.

She frowned.

"Why the frown?" He touched her cheek.

Was she frowning? Reese schooled her face, ripped off another strip of fabric from her shirt, made a pad with part of it and pressed it to his wound, maybe a little harder than she should have.

He flinched. "Mad about something?"

"This whole situation. I'm supposed to be on a diplomatic mission with Ferrence Klein, protecting him from threats, not alone in the jungle with a stranger, far from my client."

"Sometimes plans change. Missions change. You have to learn to roll with the punches."

She glanced at the nest of branches. "I'm rolling." She nodded toward the makeshift bed. "You sleep. I'm taking first watch."

"I don't need much sleep. You can go first."

Her lips curled on the corners. "Do you always argue this much? You've lost blood. You need to rest." She switched off the flashlight and remained in an upright position, refusing to lie down beside him.

Diesel could tell by the stubborn tilt of her

chin that he couldn't change her mind. Used to catching Z's wherever and whenever he had the opportunity, he'd make use of this time to refill his internal store of energy. "Have it your way. But wake me in a couple hours. You need to sleep, too. We might have a long trek ahead of us tomorrow." When he woke, he'd figure a way out of the jungle and back to his normal routine.

He lay staring up into the darkness, wide awake, wondering about this woman he'd rescued from the rebels. She wasn't like most women he knew. "How did you end up hiring on to protect Klein?"

"I had some connections," she replied.

"What's your background? What makes you qualified to protect Klein?"

She hesitated only for a moment before firing back, "What makes you qualified to recover him?" She was feisty and gave as good as she got.

Diesel chuckled. "I'm in the navy. My team was tasked with the mission to rescue you and Klein."

Silence stretched between them.

"Four years active duty in the army and two years on the MMA circuit."

"MMA?" he asked.

"Mixed Martial Arts."

"Why the army?" he asked.

"Why the navy?"

"Family legacy. My father was a marine, my grandfather was in the navy. I guess you could say it was in my blood. I like a challenge," Diesel said. "Your turn. What's your story?"

"Why do you care?" she said.

Diesel sighed. "Look, I'm just trying to get to know the woman I'm sleeping with in the jungle."

Again, she was quiet for a few moments before speaking. "My parents died in car wreck a few days after I graduated high school. I had nothing keeping me there, no home to go to. A recruiter said, *Join the army, see the world.* So, I did."

"But you didn't stay in the army."

"No." The one word was spoken in a tight, sharp tone.

"Deploy?"

"Yes. And when I got off active duty, I became an MMA fighter."

Diesel stopped suddenly, his brows rising. "Seriously?" He touched her arm. An MMA fighter was the last thing he expected to come from her mouth. "I mean, you're in great shape and all, but I didn't picture you as someone who'd fight for sport. Why the MMA?" he asked.

"I had some anger management issues I needed to resolve." She shifted. "Are you finished with the interrogation?"

"I am."

"Good, because you're supposed to be sleeping."

Diesel suspected there was a lot more to Reese's story than she was sharing, but he wouldn't push her more. If she wanted him to know more, she'd tell him. He had enough to go on, for now.

He'd hoped talking would make him less aware of her tight body. When she'd been in his lap, he'd been so turned on, he'd thought for sure she'd notice. Her body was honed, her attitude determined, but she was vulnerable enough to make him want to protect her. And if that meant holding her in his arms through the night, so be it. He swallowed a groan on that last thought. Maybe it was a good thing they split the watch and slept in shifts. Nowhere in his life did he have room to fall for the long-legged, curvaceous bodyguard, even if she was pretty hot in the red glow of the flashlight. And she had gumption. No. He needed to complete this mission and move on.

He lay on his back, unable to ignore the warmth of her thigh pressed against his. Swallowing a groan, he focused on sleep. He'd never had trouble falling asleep before he'd met Reese. Why start now?

Chapter Four

Reese sat beside Diesel in the nest of boughs and stared through the gaps in the camouflage he'd applied to the netting. Every time the man moved, he brushed up against her, making her heart race and her body light up. What was wrong with her? Even if she wanted, she couldn't begin to sleep with her thoughts running wild over her rescuer.

When Diesel had flashed his smile and winked at Reese, butterflies had erupted and swarmed in her belly, and heat had spread from her center outward. Not only was the man as hard as a bodybuilder, he was charming and sexy, too. A triple threat to her libido. She shook her head. She was in a tree, in a jungle with a man she'd met only a few hours ago. How could she be having lascivious thoughts about him when they were both covered in sweat and dirt?

She could hear the steady breathing of the man beside her. Darkness kept her from studying him. Time passed slowly with nothing but her thoughts to keep her company. Every sound made her tense up until her back ached. In the wee hours of the morning, her head dipped, and sleep threatened to overtake her.

She didn't want to wake Diesel. He was the one who was wounded. His body needed time to recover.

Guilt made a knot in her gut. She'd already botched her first assignment. Ferrence's father would fire her as soon as she got back to civilization. She wouldn't have a job, and word-of-mouth about her failure would see to it she never had another bodyguard client. The least she could do was watch over the navy SEAL.

But she was so darned sleepy.

The man lying beside her moved. A second later, a hand touched her shoulder, and Diesel pressed the drinking tube against her fingers. "Drink and then sleep."

She didn't argue. Too tired to do anything but what he commanded, she sipped from the tube, the liquid soothing her dry throat. Then she lay on the bows and closed her eyes.

Reese must have fallen asleep right away. When she opened her eyes, she could make out all the shapes and shadows within the nest Diesel had created.

One thing she couldn't see was the man himself.

Reese bolted upright and listened for the reassuring sound of him moving around outside the mosquito netting.

She heard sounds, but they weren't the sounds she expected. Something was moving down below—a lot of somethings. And there were several grunts and other sounds she couldn't quite place. She leaned forward and pressed her face to the netting. In the clearing below, dark shapes moved about. Some big, some smaller, but none of them human.

Her heart leaped into her throat, and she fought back a gasp.

A troop of gorillas had moved into the clearing and appeared to be setting up camp. Even from her perch high above them, Reese could tell they were big. Mothers sat preening their babies. Adolescent gorillas romped in the clearing, wrestling and tumbling.

Reese looked for the alpha male but didn't see him. He had to be there. All troops had an alpha male, and the alpha could be extremely fierce.

Where was Diesel?

"Shh," came a soft whisper close to her ear.

The sound was so quiet, she almost didn't hear it. Reese turned toward Diesel on the other side of the mosquito net.

He pointed down and mouthed the words *alpha male*.

Reese gulped. She worried that, if the alpha male caught their scent, he could climb the tree and rip them apart. Holy hell. And she thought being caught by Congolese rebels was bad. At least they hadn't been capable of ripping her apart with their bare hands. There would be no reasoning with a male gorilla.

Reese remained still, afraid to move and disturb the branches of the nest Diesel had built. Thankfully, they were at least twenty-five feet from the floor of the jungle. More importantly, they were twenty-five feet from the male gorilla. At the very least, they had a head start at climbing higher.

Her heart raced and her hands grew clammy. How good would she be climbing if her hands were slick with nervous sweat?

Silence and minimal movement were the orders of the day. Reese settled back and observed the social structure of the troop. Never had she ever imagined she'd have a front-row seat at a family gathering of giant apes.

They ate, groomed and dozed in the morning heat, in no hurry to move on to a different area. The strong scent of their bodies drifted upward to where Reese sat, but she didn't let that bother her. The social dynamics of the group of gorillas was fascinating.

For a couple of hours, the gorillas sat. Reese grew uncomfortable and needed to relieve herself, but she didn't dare move. She wondered how much longer the troop would be in the area.

Suddenly, the bigger gorillas sent out a disturbed cry. Mothers gathered their offspring and herded them to the other side of the clearing, disappearing into the jungle. The male gorilla left his position beneath their tree and powered out into the center of the clearing.

Men erupted from the shadows, yelling and firing AK-47s, aiming for the larger gorillas.

Reese gasped. "What are they doing?"

Diesel's lips pressed together. "Poachers. Gorilla hands and feet sell for a lot of money on the black market." He lifted his rifle into his hands and straightened from his position next to the nest. "Stay down."

Her heart grinding to a stop, Reese stared from Diesel to the men below. "What are you going to do?"

"I'm going to stop the carnage."

"But they outnumber you. You'll be killed."

"They don't know I'm here." He slipped off the limb and lowered himself to the one below, moving away from where Reese hunkered low against the branch, wishing she had a weapon.

The smallest gorillas screamed and ran ahead of their mothers. The alpha male ran toward the two men bearing weapons closest to him, roaring loud enough to make the leaves shake in the trees.

Before the men could yank their rifles up, the gorilla swept out a mighty hand and knocked the two men across the clearing.

Once the other men realized what was happening, they turned their rifles toward the huge silverback and fired.

With every bullet that hit the big ape, Reese flinched. The gorilla had done nothing to deserve this attack. Even though he could just as easily have killed her and Diesel, he hadn't, and all he was doing was protecting his troop.

Reese pressed a hand to her chest as the big gorilla charged the men shooting at him. In her heart, Reese hoped the big ape killed the men trying to kill him. It would serve them right for what they were doing to the endangered species. She wished she still had a gun.

A yell suspiciously similar to the ones from the old Tarzan movies sounded below, and shots rang out from beneath the tree in which Reese hid. Diesel, covered in leaves and camouflage, charged out of the shadows, firing his M4A1 rifle. He ran toward the group of poachers like a creature straight from hell.

"Are you insane?" Reese shoved aside the netting and climbed out on the limb. "You'll get your fool-self killed."

The group of men hadn't expected the gorillas to fire back at them. Apparently, they were so stunned by Diesel's appearance, they shot rounds into the air on reflex, then turned and ran into the jungle.

The huge gorilla spun around and roared in Diesel's direction, but the man had already ducked into the brush, completely blending into the foliage.

Blood oozed from the gorilla's wounds, but he was able to run after his troop, into the woods.

Minutes later, the clearing was empty and nothing moved.

Reese counted to fifty, praying Diesel hadn't been hit by a stray bullet. Why wasn't he coming back to the tree?

Then she noticed a movement at the far end of the clearing, where the two men had been knocked out by the male gorilla.

They rose, grabbed their weapons and spoke to each other in hushed tones. Then they walked around the clearing, their rifles held out in front of them, ready to shoot anything that moved.

Reese stared at the two. They were both dark-skinned—possibly Congolese. And one of them had on a shirt she remembered from her time in captivity with the rebels. She wondered if these thugs could be the same people who'd captured her and Ferrence?

She remained still, refusing to move a muscle. Since she could see them clearly, they could potentially see her, if they looked up.

The two men frowned, shrugged and

started in the direction the others had gone, when suddenly a twig fell from the tree below where Reese hovered.

The men spun around and aimed their weapons up at the branches.

Reese knew the exact second the man in the shirt she recognized spotted her. His eyes widened, and he said something to the man beside him. Then he tipped his rifle upward, aiming directly at her.

The man beside him did the same.

With no way to protect herself, she stood transfixed.

A shot rang out and then another.

Reese braced herself for pain, but none came. She pressed her hand to her racing heart and stared at the ground.

Then the two men below crumpled to the ground below her, their weapons falling from their hands. They lay still.

Finally, Diesel emerged from the brush, but followed the shadows up to the point he had to step out into the open to check the two men.

"They're dead, but their buddies might circle back to check on what the gunfire was all about." He glanced up at her in the tree. "Need help getting down?"

She shook her head. Sure, she was still petrified of heights, but what had just happened was more intense than getting out of a tree. She worked her way down, slipping from limb to limb, until she reached the last one. Then she dropped to the ground and ran to where Diesel stood over the bodies of the two men.

"Are they dead?"

"Very." He drew in a deep breath. "We need to keep moving."

"Do you think the male gorilla will survive?"

He shook his head. "I don't know. He took quite a few hits. But he's a big guy. Hopefully he'll make it."

Reese hoped so, too. She stared at Diesel's arm. "That was a reckless stunt. You could have been killed."

He grinned. "Would you have missed me?"

"Yes, damn it. You're supposed to be rescuing me, not ditching me in the jungle. And you're bleeding again." She started to rip the hem of her shirt again, but his hand stopped her.

"You won't have anything left of your shirt at that rate." He shed the vest with the metal plate and his outer shirt, then he pulled the black T-shirt from the waistband of his pants. "You can use this." He yanked the T-shirt over his head and handed it to her. Then he reached into a scabbard on his calf and handed her a knife.

Her heart thudding against her ribs, Reese focused on slicing off the bottom four inches of the shirt, refusing to focus on Diesel's naked, tanned chest. If she thought his muscles were sexy in the shirt… Reese dragged in a shaky breath and let it out slowly. The man had no idea what he was doing to her libido. His being hot, sweaty and covered in jungle grime didn't put a dent in his appeal. If anything, it made him appear even more rugged and badass.

Her hand slipped, and she almost cut the tip of her finger.

"Hey." Diesel grabbed her hand and the knife. "Careful. One person injured is more than enough."

"It's okay. It didn't break the skin."

"I'll be the judge of that." He studied the finger and then lifted it to his lips.

Reese's breath caught in her lungs, and her eyes widened.

Diesel kissed her fingertip and winked. "You're right. You'll live."

Only if she remembered how to breathe. Reese pulled her finger out of his grip and glanced down at the T-shirt. What was it she was doing? Oh, yes. She was playing combat medic to Diesel's wound.

His hands closed around hers. "Want me to do it?"

"No," she said. "No. You can't dress your own arm." She shook her head free of her lusty thoughts and directed her attention to Diesel's arm. The skin around the wound was an angry red, and the sore oozed. "We have to get you to a doctor ASAP. This gunshot wound is infected."

"I'm all for finding a doctor, only I'm not sure where to start." When she finished binding his arm, he shrugged into his shirt and stuffed the tail into his trousers.

Reese folded the remainder of his T-shirt and tucked it into her blouse for use later, if needed.

A finger touched her beneath her chin and tipped her head up. Her gaze skimmed across his lips, noticing how full and firm they were. Dragging her glance from his mouth, she stared into Diesel's eyes.

Bad move. She hoped he couldn't tell what she was thinking by where her gaze had lingered. At that moment, she wanted nothing more than to kiss the man.

"Thank you for taking care of me," he whispered. His head lowered, his lips hovering over hers. "I can't help it. I have this insane urge to kiss you." And he did. His mouth claimed hers in a deep, mind-melding kiss that rocked Reese to her very core. She'd placed her hands on his chest, but they found their way to the back of his neck, pulling him closer.

The jungle, the bugs, killer animals and dangerous men faded into the background as she pressed her body to his.

His tongue darted out, skimming the seam of her lips, urging her to open. When she did, he slipped his tongue inside, caressing her tongue with his in a long, sensuous swirl.

When at last Diesel lifted his head, Reese's head was spinning. Her thoughts fogged, and she dragged in a steadying breath. She wiped the back of her hand over her swollen, pulsing lips. "Why did you do that?"

He chuckled. "I've wanted to since I found you in the rebel camp." Diesel brushed her cheek with the tips of his fingers. "I'd kiss you again, but we need to move before those jokers return." Diesel, dressed in his shirt and vest, took her hand and led her out of the clearing, heading north again.

Reese hurried alongside him, pulse racing, heart tight in her chest and lips tingling from his kiss. What had started as an escape from enemy territory had almost changed into an exotic adventure with a man whose mere presence made her body burn with desire.

How could this be? They were in a life-or-death situation where anything could kill them, from raging hippos to angry rebels. Not to mention, they could die of starvation or dehydration, infection or disease before they found some form of civilization where they could seek medical attention. And here she was thinking about what else was beneath the clothes this man wore.

Hell, she didn't even know him!

Pushing hard to keep up with him, Reese didn't have much breath available to ask questions, but she tried. "So, what exactly is this team of yours? Army, navy, marines?"

"If I tell you—"

"You'll have to kill me." She sucked in a deep breath and double-timed to keep up with his longer stride. "Cut to the chase. I'm in this with you, and I can keep a secret."

"We're navy SEALs."

That would explain why he was so well trained and in remarkable physical condition. Whew. Not only was he hot, he was one of America's elite forces. Wow. Talk about every woman's dream—to be swept off her feet by a navy SEAL. And she'd been swept off her feet more than once. Well, she couldn't let that happen again. Navy SEALs were bad boyfriend material, and even worse at marriage. Not that she was thinking about marrying the man. Hell, she hadn't even had a date since she'd been released by the Taliban. She hadn't really been interested in men, and wasn't sure she ever would be again. A relationship with Diesel was completely out of the question. Reese marched forward, determined to keep her head out of the clouds and her feet firmly on the ground.

DIESEL COULD TELL his revelation about being a navy SEAL wasn't welcomed by his jungle escape partner. Most women found it exciting to be with a SEAL. Why was Reese different? He realized he didn't know much about the woman he'd rescued from the Congolese rebels. "What made you become a bodyguard?" He glanced down at her. "Don't tell me it was a dream of yours as a little girl."

She shook her head and stared at the path in front of her. "No. I kind of fell into it."

"You're in good physical shape. You had to have worked up to that."

Reese shrugged and kept moving. "The physical regimen kept me sane. I had some things to work out of my system." Her voice was tight, her body stiff.

Diesel wasn't going to let her end her life history on a statement like that. "For instance?"

She walked faster, as if she were being chased by demons. And maybe she was. Diesel had a few demons of his own. A SEAL didn't live through so many battles without something bad plaguing his nightmares.

He reached out and snagged her arm, bringing her to a stop.

"We need to keep going," she said, pulling away from him.

Diesel didn't release her. "What are you running from, Reese?"

"None of your business. And who said I was running?" She jerked her arm free of his hold and glared up at him, defiantly.

He cupped her face, his heart tightening. She'd been hurt. "Whatever it was, I'm sorry it happened."

She slapped his hand away. "Why should you be sorry? You didn't do it. The filthy Taliban did it. And I swore I'd never let anyone capture me again, but it happened." She sucked in deep breaths, blowing them out through her mouth. The color was high in her cheeks, and her eyes shone with moisture. "I swore," she whispered.

Diesel cursed and pulled her into his arms. "Babe, whatever they did is done. You're a wonderful person and a strong woman."

"Not strong enough," she said into his shirt, her fingers curling into his chest. "And not strong enough to keep those men from taking me this time. What do I have to do? Where a suit of armor, rigged to electrify anyone who lays a hand on me?"

Diesel chuckled. "I for one am glad you're not wearing an electrified suit of armor." He held her at arm's length and stared down into her eyes. "You don't have to tell me what happened unless you want. I'll just know that you were hurt, and I'll do everything in my power to keep you safe from harm."

She shook her head, a single tear rolling down her cheek. "But you don't get it. I should be capable of defending myself. Otherwise, what was all of this good for?

Mixed martial arts are only good if you're conscious."

"Is that what happened? You were knocked unconscious?" He hugged her again, running his hands down her back. "You can't always plan on being conscious, can you? But I'll bet that if you had been conscious, they'd have wished you were out cold. You'd have given them a run for their money."

Reese drew in several deep breaths and pushed away from Diesel. "Sorry. I haven't had a meltdown in a long time."

"You call that a meltdown?" Diesel laughed. "Far from it. Most women I know scream, kick and sob buckets of tears in a meltdown."

She sniffed and tilted her chin up. "I'm not most women."

"I'm beginning to understand that about you. And I like it." He held out his hand. "Ready to find civilization?"

"More than ready." She hesitated before placing her hand in his.

Together, they set off, moving upriver. The heat was debilitating, and they soon ran out of drinking water. With all the water flowing beside them in the Congo, they didn't dare drink it.

Though she put up a good front, Reese was slowing down. Lack of food and fluid was taking its toll on her and on Diesel, as well.

He worried that if they didn't find help soon...well, he didn't want to think about the alternative.

Several times, they strayed too close to the riverbanks and had to hurry out of the way of giant crocodiles and wading hippos. The sun hit its zenith and plunged toward the opposite horizon, and still they hadn't found a village or other people.

Just about the time Diesel was considering where they would sleep that night, he spied someone in a dugout canoe, paddling by on the river. Hope surged through him, and he stopped, bringing Reese close beside him. He ducked, staring through the branches to the river beyond. "See that?"

She nodded.

"He's not in a motorized boat. He can't be too far from a village."

She sighed. "That would great, as long as the villagers are friendly, and the village is on this side of the river."

"We'll have to ease up on it before we announce ourselves." Diesel set off, moving with more care and an awareness that they could walk right out of the jungle and into a village before they realized it. The jungle often crept in on villages if they didn't fight it back on a regular basis. Nature had a way of reclaiming what was hers.

Twenty minutes later, people's voices and the hum of a generator were like sounds from heaven. Diesel pressed a finger to his lips. They were in luck. The sound was on their side of the river.

Reese nodded and followed him, doing what he did, moving from shadow to shadow, until they stood at the edge of an encampment scraped out of the jungle. A dock had been erected, jutting out into the river. Several small skiffs with outboard motors were tied to the jetty, and canoes lay beached on the banks nearby. People moved about the small village, some carrying what appeared to be bags of grain. Others had handmade baskets filled with a variety of fruits and vegetables.

Diesel's mouth watered, but he didn't dare step out of the jungle until he knew for certain they were not in danger.

Reese tugged on his shirt and pointed to the far side of the village, where a large white tent had been erected with the words MEDI-

CINS SANS FRONTIERES written across the sides. She grinned at him and mouthed the word "Bingo."

An older woman with white hair, wearing blue jeans, a T-shirt and a yellow-and-white jacket stepped out of the tent and stretched her back, staring out at the river.

Diesel backed away from the village, far enough that their voices wouldn't carry. "We need to get to that tent. Hopefully, whoever that woman is speaks English and can tell us how to get a ride out of here."

Reese nodded.

"Follow me." Diesel led the way, making a wide circle around the camp, coming up from behind the medical tent. He couldn't see straight into the tent. The back was closed off, with only the front opening for an entrance.

Fortunately, the white-haired woman stepped around the tent with a bucket of water and walked toward the jungle. Just as she swung her arms back to empty the bucket, Diesel spoke. "Hey, do you speak English?"

The woman yelped, dropped the bucket and stepped backward. "Who said that?"

Reese stood, exposing her position to the

woman. "We did. Hi, I'm Reese and this is Diesel."

Diesel rose to stand beside her. "Ma'am, are you American?"

She nodded, pressing a hand to her breast. "You scared the bejeezus out of me." The woman frowned. "I'm Martha Kowalski. And yes, I'm American. Why are you hiding in the jungle?"

"My friend was held captive by Congolese rebels. I helped her escape, and they might be looking for us." Diesel glanced behind the woman.

The woman looked over her shoulder and back to Diesel and Reese. "You're right to worry. We've had to be very careful. If it weren't for the fact they need us here so badly, I'm sure we would be in more danger than we are. How can I help you?"

Reese spoke before Diesel. "He's been shot and needs medical attention." She pointed to the bloody scrap of T-shirt on his arm.

The woman moved closer, frowning. "We have the medications and bandages you'll need. But to get you into the tent to take care of it will alert the village to your presence." She bit her bottom lip and narrowed her eyes. "Wait here. I have an idea."

Diesel and Reese ducked low into the foliage and waited for the woman's return.

Several minutes passed. Diesel began to think she wasn't coming back or had run into trouble. But then she appeared around the side of the tent, carrying an armful of packages. A man followed her, just as old and white-haired as the woman, carrying more sealed packages.

They walked into the jungle and kept going until they were well outside the perimeter of the camp. Diesel and Reese followed.

"Reese, Diesel, this is my husband, Dr. Jerry Kowalski."

The man nodded and set his packages on the ground. "These suits will get you into the tents, past the other patients and their families, no questions asked."

They tore into the sealed packages to discover personal protective suits. "We had these shipped in recently because there have been several reported cases of the Ebola virus. We use these suits to protect medical staff from patients infected with highly contagious diseases or viruses."

Diesel grinned. "And they will cover us from head to toe." He reached for one of the packages and winced. He hadn't said anything to Reese, but his arm had become increasingly sore and achy over the past few hours. He suspected infection had set in. He handed one of the suits to Reese. "Suit up." The sooner he got the arm treated, the sooner they could be on their way back to civilization and safety.

Then he and Reese would part ways. Somehow, that end goal didn't make him happy. He'd dated other women, but none he'd considered going out with more than once or twice. Reese would have been another story. He could see spending time with her and enjoying it. But what else could he do? His job would be done, and she had hers to resume.

Chapter Five

Reese pulled the yellow-and-white jump-suit of synthetic fabric up over her legs, hips and torso, then pushed her arms through the sleeves.

Diesel seemed to struggle into his, barely using his injured arm.

Reese suspected the wound was infected and could turn septic if they didn't get it cleaned out and fill him with antibiotics quickly.

Martha held up a hand. "Wait." She helped him remove the shirt and the bandage, exposing the wound. She clucked her tongue and shook her head. "We need to tend to it immediately." She helped him into the suit and slipped the head gear over his face.

Martha and Dr. Kowalski suited up, as well.

Once they were all fully covered, the four

of them walked out into the open, led by Martha and Jerry. They walked around to the front of the tent and entered.

Cots lined the walls inside, and a section in the very back was blocked off by walls of waterproof tent material with a zippered door as an entrance. Martha unzipped the door and held it to the side as Dr. Kowalski, Diesel and Reese entered. Martha entered behind them and zipped the door shut again. No one could see in or out of the small area.

As quickly as they could, Martha and Dr. Kowalski shed their protective suits and went to work. Martha switched on a battery-powered light hanging from the ceiling and set up a tray of medical equipment, gauze and a bottle of clear saline solution. Dr. Kowalski washed his hands, slipped into a surgical shirt and mask and stepped up to Diesel. "Have a seat." He indicated the end of the cot with a tilt of his head.

Diesel didn't argue. His wound was hurting, the pain radiating throughout his arm.

As a former soldier, Reese knew as well as anyone what happened to wounds that were left untreated. She hoped they weren't too late to fight the infection.

The doctor irrigated the site and cleaned

it thoroughly. Martha handed him what he needed, without having to be asked. They worked well as a team. When they had the site completely cleaned of dirt, dried blood and pus, Dr. Kowalski sewed the skin shut, applied a bandage and held it in place with adhesive tape.

"Now lie down," Martha said.

Diesel obeyed.

Martha set him up with an IV of clear liquid and added something to the tube.

He frowned. "You're not giving me a sedative, are you?" he whispered, careful not to let his voice carry beyond the thin walls of the tent.

She shook her head. "No. Just an antibiotic to ward off infection. You need to have your wits around you if those rebels show up in the village."

He smiled at the woman and her husband and mouthed the words "Thank you."

The smile melted everything at Reese's core. She had to turn away to keep him from seeing how it affected her by the heat rising in her face.

Martha patted his shoulder. "The fluids will help keep you from dehydration." She glanced at Reese. "I'll bring you water and food. In the meantime, you look like you could use some rest." She switched off the overhead light, plunging the room into darkness.

Reese hadn't realized how late it had gotten.

Martha and the doctor dressed in their protective suits and left the isolation room, zipping the door behind them. A faint light shined through the thin tent wall.

Reese scooted a cot close to Diesel and lay on her side, staring across at him, wanting to be near him. "Feel better?"

"I will when the infection dies down." He pressed his lips together. "We can't stay here long."

"I know. But let the antibiotics get into your bloodstream and the additional fluids. Then we can decide what to do next."

Diesel held out his free hand, capturing hers. "Are you sure you're all right?"

She snorted. "I'm fine. A few blisters and a little heat rash, but nothing a bath and a pedicure won't fix." She winked.

"I can't imagine an MMA fighter getting a pedicure."

She laughed softly, though her heart was flip-flopping at the way his fingers rubbed hers. "You'd be surprised what's required. Not only did we have to have our hair and makeup perfect, but we had to have neatly manicured nails. We had to look good while we pounded each other's faces into the mats."

He touched a finger to the tip of her nose. "Is that why your nose is crooked? Not that it isn't cute, but I wondered."

She stiffened. "No." Her nose had been broken by the Taliban.

"Was it always crooked?"

"No." Reese released his hand, rolled onto her back and stared at the ceiling. The last thing she wanted to think about was her experience in Afghanistan. She prayed her current situation didn't end up similarly. Hopefully, having a navy SEAL around would help keep her safe.

"Sorry. I take it I'm stepping into no-man's land again."

She shrugged and lay for a while without speaking, breathing in and out to calm her racing heart.

DIESEL CLOSED HIS eyes and drew in a deep breath.

Reese had some baggage she carried around. Trying to talk to her about it was like walking through a minefield. He suspected she'd open up eventually, if he was patient.

His fists clenched. The men who'd captured her in Afghanistan must have done horrible things to her. He wished he could find them and strangle them with his bare hands. Any men who mistreated women were barbarians who didn't deserve to live.

Then out of the darkness, Reese's voice sounded in a barely discernible whisper. "I was a driver in a convoy transporting supplies to one of the forward operating bases, when we were surrounded by Taliban fighters.

"The first vehicle hit an IED, killing the driver, the passenger and the gunner. The explosion disabled the truck, blocking the road. I tried to turn around, but we were rushed by men carrying rifles and machine guns.

"My passenger didn't even make it out of the truck to lay down return fire before he was shot and killed. I was hit in the arm. I couldn't hold my weapon in my left hand, much less shoot straight." Her whispers grew strangled.

Diesel didn't stop her or try to offer words of encouragement. He let her talk, the darkness providing her a little anonymity. His chest tightened with each of her words. He wanted to reach out and take her into his arms and hold her until all the bad memories disappeared.

Reese was silent for a few moments. "They grabbed me and hauled me off to one of their villages deep in the hills." She snorted. "That's when the fun began."

Diesel heard the pain in her voice.

"Let's just say, they don't treat women well…" Her voice seemed to fade. Diesel almost didn't hear her when she said, "And I'll never be able to have children."

Diesel had suspected the Taliban fighters had raped and tortured her. But hearing her quiet admission about children hit him like a punch to the gut. He swallowed the bile rising in his throat, his heart aching for the young woman so badly abused by her enemy. If he could, he would have taken away all of her pain and killed every one of the bastards who'd done the damage.

She gave a harsh laugh. "I was one of the lucky ones. A Delta-Force team had targeted that village to eradicate the Taliban hiding there. They found me and took me back to the nearest medical facility. From there, I was flown back to the States, where I had an almost 'full' recovery, but I was processed out on a medical discharge for PTSD."

Diesel lay for a while, unsure of what to say. Nothing seemed appropriate, and he couldn't get up and wrap his arms around her with a blasted IV in his arm.

"I was out of the army, out of a job and angry. I vowed never to be vulnerable like that again. So, I worked out, took self-defense and martial arts lessons. One day, a woman approached me about joining the MMA circuit. She thought I had what it took to succeed in the arena. I had so much hate and anger simmering below the surface, I needed an outlet."

"That's a tough job," Diesel commented.

"You're telling me. I gave it two years. When I was tired of broken fingers, cracked ribs and having my bell rung more times than I could count, I retired and started my own bodyguard business. That's where Ferrence's father came in. He was my first, and possibly my last, client."

"You'll have more. You can't blame yourself for what happened while you were unconscious."

"Yeah, I could have insisted we avoid the situation all together."

"Hindsight is always twenty-twenty. You have to move on. Learn from your past, but leave it in the past."

She grunted. "Easy to say, not to do."

"I know." And he did. He'd lost several of his buddies in operations that had gone south. For months afterward, he second-guessed his every move during newer assignments. When it began to impact every new operation, he sought help. Not with anyone in the military. One of his friends had a wife who was a psychologist who specialized in treatment for soldiers with PTSD. She'd helped him to come to grips with his past, to allow him to move forward into this future. Without her help, he'd still be hesitating when he should be acting, and possibly costing more lives due to indecision.

To Diesel, Reese sounded like she hadn't found her way to the future. She was still beating herself up over the past, afraid to think there was a future for her.

War had a way of breaking perfectly healthy individuals.

Before Diesel could think of anything to say that would make everything better for Reese, Martha unzipped the door and entered, carrying a tray of food. Light shined in from the other tent compartment. Martha still wore the protective gear and remained in it until she closed the zippered door.

She reached for the overhead light, turned it on and set the tray on the end of Reese's bed.

Reese sat up.

When Diesel also tried to sit up, Martha shook her head. "Lay still. I'll bring it to you."

"You don't have to wait on us. We're hungry and able-bodied," Diesel reassured her, careful not to talk too loudly.

"You need to let the antibiotics do their job," Martha warned him.

"Right now, food is as important as the antibiotics." Reese licked her lips, staring at the crackers and peanut butter Martha proffered.

Other items were packaged like the US Army's Meals Ready to Eat or MREs. Even those sounded good at that point.

Diesel's mouth watered.

"Go ahead, then." Martha smiled. "Eat and then rest. The doctor and I will keep watch."

Reese grabbed for a cracker, slathered peanut butter over the surface and handed it to Diesel.

He waited until she had one for herself and then bit into it like it was a delicacy.

"I'd offer you some of the local cuisine, but I'm not certain your bellies could handle it right now. Eat what's there, and I'll get more."

"Mrs. Martha," Diesel said.

"Yes?"

"Is there a way to get to a larger town? One with a telephone or a cell phone tower?"

Martha nodded. "The boat comes once a week, carrying supplies and mail. You're in luck. It's due to arrive tomorrow."

Diesel glanced over at Reese. "Do you think we can barter for passage on the boat?"

"Certainly. It's how we got here and how the locals get to and from the market upriver. Do you have any Congolese currency?"

Diesel smiled. "As a matter of fact, I do." He reached into a pocket of his cargo pants and pulled out a plastic bag filled with different currency notes.

Reese chuckled. "Another item from your survival kit?"

He grinned. "Absolutely. You never know when you have to bribe your way out of a situation."

Martha smiled. "You are a resourceful man."

"I try," Diesel said. "Will this be enough?"

Martha thumbed through the bills, separated a few and held them up. "Don't offer more than this. If they know you have more, they'll charge you more." The older woman checked Diesel's IV, fussed over his bandages and then slipped her hood back on and left the compartment.

Diesel and Reese didn't talk for the next few minutes. Instead, they ate, concentrating on filling their empty stomachs.

Martha had gone to the trouble of heating some of the packages. Diesel found one of macaroni and cheese and ate every last bite.

Reese dug into one marked beef stew.

When they'd eaten their fill, Diesel lay back on the cot and stared up at the light dangling from the ceiling. "I didn't realize just how hungry I was."

"Me either." Reese lay down beside him, closed her eyes and yawned.

"You should sleep. You heard our host. Martha and the doctor will warn us if the rebels find their way to this village."

"At this point, I'm not sure I could keep my

eyes open." Reese yawned again and tucked her hand beneath her cheek.

Diesel stared over at her, admiring the way her lashes formed dark crescents beneath her eyes. She'd kept up with his grueling pace and hadn't complained. She'd been through hell and back on more than one occasion and hadn't cracked. Reese was one tough cookie. *On the outside.* But she was soft and vulnerable on the inside.

"Diesel?" she whispered.

"Yeah, sweetheart?" he answered.

"What I told you," she yawned, "I don't want anyone feeling sorry for me. I'm okay. And I never told anyone else."

"Gotcha." Diesel's gut clenched. "Your secret is safe with me."

"Thanks," she said on a sigh. Soon the sound of her steady breathing let him know she'd fallen asleep.

He watched her until his own eyelids drooped. He needed sleep as much as she did to continue their journey.

Diesel reached across to the other cot and took Reese's hand in his. For now, all he wanted to do was hold on to this amazing woman. Tomorrow, they'd be on their way toward civilization and freedom.

Reese woke with a start. She lay for a moment, trying to determine what had disturbed her sleep.

Shouts outside the tent made her jerk to a sitting position. Light through the tent panel from the other compartment gave the room a deep gray, just-past-dusk feeling. She could see well enough, but not all the nuances.

Diesel was off the cot and standing in two seconds flat, ripping the IV from his arm. He touched her shoulder. "Sounds like we might have company. There's a raid on the village."

Gunshots were fired outside. Men yelled. Women and children screamed in the night.

Diesel dragged the rifle out from beneath the cot, as the zipper on their compartment was yanked up. He aimed at the intruder only to lower his rifle when a woman's white head poked inside.

Martha's eyes were rounded, her face flushed. "Suit up. They're headed this way. Dr. Kowalski won't be able to hold them off for long." She already wore the protective suit without the hood. She nodded toward the pile she'd placed in the corner. "If they come in, look like you're half-dead. I'll make an excuse for a patient to be in a suit. Just don't talk."

"Yes, ma'am," Reese said. She grabbed a suit and jammed her feet into the legs, pulling the jumpsuit up her torso as quickly as possible. Once she had hers on, she helped Diesel into his. She'd just settled the hood over his head, when loud voices sounded from the entrance to the tent.

Reese slipped her hood over her head and lay on the cot.

Diesel lay on the other, his rifle tucked beneath his leg, completely covered by the baggy synthetic fabric.

"You can't go in there. Those patients are infected with the deadly Ebola virus," Dr. Kowalski said.

"We will go where we please," a deeply accented voice said.

"Let him go, Dr. Kowalski. It's his life. If he wants to die of Ebola, let him," Martha said. She unzipped the compartment and held back the flap door. "Go. See for yourself."

Reese lowered her eyelids almost all of the way. She could just see through the slits.

A big black man with a camouflage outfit and a vest filled with loaded magazines leaned through the doorway with two others similarly attired. He stopped short of entering. Instead, he brandished his rifle at

Reese and Diesel. "Why are they wearing these clothes?"

Dr. Kowalski stepped up beside Martha. "The two in there are hyper-contagious, we had to put them in suits to protect the other patients from getting the virus. They come from a village where all the other people have perished."

"Perished? What is this?" the rebel demanded.

"Died," Martha cried. "They all died." Then she turned and sobbed against Dr. Kowalski's chest. "Every last man, woman and child are gone from their village."

"Then why are they here? Why didn't you leave them to die with their people?" the rebel demanded.

"We couldn't leave them," Dr. Kowalski said. "They were still breathing. Our jobs are to help those in need, no matter how sick."

"You should shoot them so they don't infect everyone else along the river." The rebel raised his rifle.

Reese tensed. She had no weapon to defend herself. If Diesel pulled out his rifle, they'd have all the other rebels on top of them in seconds.

A shout from outside made the man with

the gun swing around. "Get them out of here. They shouldn't be around to infect the others."

"We'll do our best," the doctor promised.

"And if you see a white man and woman pass through this area, you are to send word to us immediately. Do you understand?"

Martha sobbed, and Dr. Kowalski nodded, holding her close to him. "We understand."

Then the man with the gun was gone, taking his sidekicks with him.

Diesel rose to his feet, ripped off the hood and held his rifle at the ready.

Reese realized that if the rebel leader and his goons returned, they might not get a second chance. Again, she wished she had a weapon of her own.

As if he'd read her mind, Diesel reached into a pocket and pulled out a small pistol. "Hang on to this. It won't stop an eight-hundred-pound gorilla, but it could ruin a man's day if he tries to hurt you."

She clutched the pistol, ejected the magazine in the handle and slammed it back into the grip. It was light and almost felt like a toy. But like Diesel said, it could ruin a man's day at close range.

Martha sobbed until the shouting outside

faded into the distance. When they were finally alone, but for the patients in the outer compartment, the doctor and his assistant entered the compartment.

Martha righted the IV stand and collected the empty bag from the floor. "You'll have to go as soon as the morning boat arrives. It usually gets here early. We're the last stop before it heads back to the closest big town. If the rebels are gone when it arrives, you should have no problem boarding. If they hang around, you might have to miss this boat and wait for the next, a week from now."

Diesel's gaze met Reese's. If she read it right, they were in agreement. They would be on that boat come hell or high water. Reese was ready to be done with the jungle, mosquitos, crocodiles and anything else that could eat her in the night. She needed to get back to Ferrence. Despite their detour, they still had a political agenda to fulfill. The time they'd set aside for his safari was nearing an end. If she had any chance at all at redeeming herself, she had to get back to civilization and back to her client, Ferrence Klein.

Martha and the doctor stripped out of their protective gear and left Diesel and Reese alone in the quarantine compartment. On the other side of the panel, the medical workers checked their patients, calming them after the rebel fighters' visit.

Soon the noise in the village ended, lights were extinguished and the little town slept.

Not Reese and Diesel. They sat on the edges of their cots, listening, waiting for the morning light of dawn and the sound of a boat engine.

THE BOAT ENGINE arrived as the gray light of predawn filtered through the white walls of the tent.

Martha and Dr. Kowalski unzipped the compartment and entered, zipping the door back up behind them.

"A different boat arrived at the dock. We think it might be American," Dr. Kowalski said.

"You might want to check it out from the safety of the jungle," Martha suggested. "Perhaps they are friends?"

Reese stood and stretched, tired to the bone, but curious. "Do you think it might be your team?"

"Maybe." Diesel tucked his rifle down the leg of his protective suit, settled the hood over his head and nodded to Reese. "Let's go see."

Reese slid the hood over her head and nodded. Together, they left the tent and rounded to the back, walking deeper into the shadowy jungle. When they were far enough away from the encampment, they stripped out of the protective gear and hurried around the perimeter to the shore of the river, keeping an eye out for crocodiles and snakes.

When they reached a position where they could see the dock, Diesel chuckled. "It's them." He started for the dock.

Reese shot out a hand. "Are you sure it's safe?"

"Sweetheart, there's enough firepower on that boat to level this village. The Congolese rebels wouldn't stand a chance against them."

Reese and Diesel walked out of the jungle and through the makeshift shelters of plywood and shipping containers that housed the villagers who lived around the dock.

A rugged-looking metal boat with machine guns mounted on all sides rested up against the dock. Several men dressed similarly to Diesel stood on the dock, rifles in hand, ready to take on anyone.

The village was just waking up.

As Diesel stepped out into the open, a couple of the men spun toward him, aiming their weapons at his chest.

Reese started to jump in front of Diesel, but the men with the guns lowered their weapons and grinned.

One stepped forward. "Diesel, you old son of a bitch, figures you'd find a way to vacation with a pretty girl." The man engulfed him in a bear hug, pounding him on the back.

"Hey, Buck." Diesel flinched and backed away, flexing his injured arm. "Watch the arm."

The man Diesel called Buck frowned. "Were you hit?"

"It's nothing, just a—"

"Flesh wound?" Buck's frown deepened. "I'll take a look at it when we get underway."

"No worries. It'll hold until we get to where we're going. The doc here patched me up and fed me antibiotics. I'm good to go."

Buck looked beyond Diesel to where Reese stood. "You must be Reese Brantley."

Reese nodded, suddenly feeling like she'd been rolling in a pigpen. She needed a shower and a change of clothing.

"We heard all about you from Klein." Another, taller man stepped up next to Buck. "I'm Jake." He held out his hand to Reese.

Wincing inwardly, she took the big man's hand and shook it. "I'm sure it was all bad."

"Not at all. He was worried about you."

"Don't lie to the lady. He was worried about who he would take with him on his political tour of Kinshasa." Another man stepped up on the other side of Buck. "Percy Taylor, but my friends call me Pitbull. And we call Jake, Big Jake, on account of his excessive height."

Reese shook the man's hand, a smile playing at her lips.

Pitbull turned to Diesel. "Thought we'd lost you, man."

Diesel shrugged. "Couldn't get back to the boat, so we took a stroll through the jungle."

Buck snorted. "Some stroll. I'm surprised you weren't eaten by a lion or crocodile."

"We were actually more worried about the poachers, our Congolese rebel kidnappers and the gorillas."

Buck's brows rose. "Gorillas?"

"Just a small troop of around twenty." Diesel gave a nonchalant shrug that almost made Reese laugh.

"No kidding?" Pitbull asked, his eyes alight. "Aren't they dangerous?"

"A little." Diesel tipped his head toward the boat. "We should be going before the rebels return. They were here earlier. And we were supposed to be in stealth mode. Why did you come now?"

"We were going for that no-man-left-behind adage," Buck said.

"Right," Pitbull added. "The team just didn't feel like it was firing on all cylinders without our Diesel."

Diesel hooked Reese's arm with his hand and guided her to the boat. He helped her aboard and stepped in after her, ushered her to a seat on a hard metal bench and then he stepped up behind one of the mounted machine guns.

"No way, man." Buck shook his head. "You're injured. You can sit this one out for now."

"I told you, it's just a flesh wound."

"Yeah, and a flesh wound in Africa can go south in a heartbeat." Buck's lips twisted. "Humor me, will ya?"

The man at the helm waited until every man on the team was aboard the boat before he turned the craft around and headed north.

"Why aren't we going back to our helicopter pickup point?" Diesel asked.

"The chopper went on to an airstrip in Zambia where a private plane will carry Klein to Kinshasa for the African Union convention. We're supposed to head down the river to the next big town. Apparently, there is a bush pilot who can take Miss Brantley the rest of the way to Kinshasa. Once we leave her there, we'll head back down the river to our previously scheduled pickup point."

"And the stealth mode?" Diesel asked.

"We hope to be off the Congo in the next twenty-four hours." Yet another one of the SEALs turned away from his position manning a machine gun. "We'll leave the cover-up for the politicians and diplomats."

Diesel settled onto the bench next to Reese, his rifle resting across his legs, one hand holding it, ready to put it to use, if the need arose.

"Navy SEALs, huh?" Reese asked, staring around at the men on the boat. "I guess that accounts for the boat."

"Not all navy SEALs are trained for riverine missions," Diesel said. "We're from a Special Boat Team. We train on these kinds of boats for missions requiring extractions via water."

Reese studied the members of the team. Each of them appeared to be fit and intent on their mission, as the boat raced along the Congo River. The helmsman maintained a steady speed, even as he rounded the curves in the winding river, skidding sideways across the surface of the water. When they came upon hippopotamuses in a wide area of the river, he skirted the beasts, giving then a wide birth. They passed canoes, dugouts and small boats with outboard motors. At one point, they passed what appeared to be the weekly supply boat, heading toward the village where Martha and Dr. Kowalski performed miracles as part of the Doctors Without Borders effort.

Three hours later, they neared a small town on the edge of the river. The jungle had been trimmed back to allow for fields of agriculture and a small airstrip.

As the fully armed boat approached the dock, people scattered, running toward town.

"Harm, Buck, Pitbull, be ready to accompany me to escort Miss Brantley to the airstrip," Big Jake said. "A plane will be waiting to take her to Kinshasa."

Diesel stood. "I'm going with her."

"Stand down, Diesel," Big Jake said. "You're in no condition to provide for her protection."

"I'm going," Diesel insisted.

To be honest, Reese wanted him to come. They'd been together for the past couple days. Going on without him would feel strange. But then, she wasn't in Africa because she needed protection. She was there to protect Ferrence Klein.

Reese laid a hand on Diesel's arm. "It's okay. These men can escort me to the airfield. I'll be all right."

Diesel touched her cheek. "You're my responsibility. I'm going." He glared at Big Jake and stepped off the boat onto the dock. Then he held out his hand to Reese.

She rested hers in his and let him assist her off the boat. Harm, Pitbull and Buck, armed with rifles, gathered around the two, and they moved as a unit across the dock and through the small town, to the field on the edge where a small plane awaited. Three armed men stood guard around the aircraft. A person wearing jeans, a white polo shirt and a baseball cap pushed away from the side of the plane.

As Reese and the team closed the distance between them, she realized the person in the jeans was a woman with long sandy hair pulled back in a ponytail behind her.

The woman held out her hand. "Hi, I'm Marly Simpson, your pilot."

Reese almost laughed at the expression on Diesel's face.

He was practically scowling at the woman. "You're the pilot?"

She nodded, her lips twisting into a wry grimace. "I am. Got a problem with it?"

Pitbull chuckled. "Only if you don't know how to fly the plane."

She shot a glare at him. "I have over twenty-five hundred hours flying in this plane and others. You're welcome to review my logbooks." Her gaze darted around the landing strip. "I suggest we get this plane in the sky. The longer it sits on the ground, the more chance of it being shot at, hijacked or stolen."

Reese tensed, her belly knotting. "You've had that happen?"

Marly sighed. "More times than you can imagine." She planted her fists on her hips and stared at the group. "Because I have a load of cargo, I can only take three passengers and no luggage. Who's coming?"

Reese stepped forward. "As far as I know, I'm the only passenger." It was time to say goodbye to her rescuer. Diesel was an integral part of the military. Surely he had better things to do than escort her around the Democratic Republic of the Congo. She turned to thank him. "Diesel, thank you for getting me out of the jungle alive." She held out her hand to shake his, her heart clenching in her chest. "Without you and your men, who knows what would have happened to Ferrence. Thank you."

He took her hand and refused to let go.

Chapter Six

With Reese pretty much telling him to shove off, Diesel's pulse rocketed. Before he could think through his decision, he said, "You're welcome. But I'm coming, too."

"What the hell?" Buck sputtered. "That's not part of the plan."

"I'm not letting them go without someone to ride shotgun," Diesel said. "You heard Marly, the plane and the people in it are subject to being hijacked. I'm not turning Reese loose without an escort all the way to Kinshasa."

Buck stared at the men guarding the plane. "What about them?"

Marly followed his gaze. "They're only contracted for guarding this airstrip. They're not coming with me."

As far as Diesel was concerned, Marly's words sealed the deal. "I'll find my way back to Djibouti. I'm not ditching Miss Brantley now. We've come too far together for me to walk away."

"I can take care of myself," Reese insisted.

"You're not in the States," Buck argued. "This is the DRC. The current government is run by a tyrant refusing to allow democratic elections. He could imprison you without cause and no chance for a trial."

Reese lifted her chin. "I'm here on a diplomatic mission and to protect Ferrence Klein, not to have you or anyone else protect me."

"Tough," Diesel said. "I'm coming with you. End of argument."

Marly frowned at them. "Please tell me you aren't going to argue the entire trip?"

"We aren't." Reese crossed her arms over her chest. "Because he's not coming with me."

"Do you always argue this much?" Diesel shook his head and gripped her arm. "Sweetheart, we've come too far together. I can't just let go. I need to know you're safe. You'd do the same if the situation was reversed."

Reese stared into his eyes, her mouth pressed into a thin line. After a moment, her stance relaxed and the corners of her lips twisted into a wry smile. "Given all that's happened, I would appreciate someone having my back." She glanced at the members of his team. "But what about your team?"

"They have to get the boat back to the pickup point. They'll need all men on deck in case they run into trouble." Diesel looked to Big Jake for concurrence.

"Right." Big Jake shook his head. "We just got you back with the team, but I get it. We'll get the SOC-R back to the rendezvous location and ship it back to Djibouti. I'll work with the commander to cover your sorry ass. But once you get to Kinshasa, you need to hightail back to Djibouti. My bet is there's another mission awaiting our attention."

Diesel drew in a deep breath and let go. He was pushing the envelope on his duty to the current mission and his loyalty to his unit. But he just couldn't let Reese leave without an armed escort. "Now that everything's settled…" He clapped his hands together. "Let's go."

The pilot climbed into the plane and took her position behind the yoke.

"I'll sit in back since you're the only one carrying a high-powered weapon," Reese volunteered.

Diesel handed Reese up into the seat behind the pilot and then laid his rifle in the front seat, before stepping up into the plane. He winced when he reached for the safety harness and pulled it across his shoulder.

Reese leaned forward. "Are you sure you're up to this? You haven't given your arm a chance to heal."

"I'm fine," he said through gritted teeth, as pain rippled through him.

"About the gun…" Marly's eyes narrowed. "You'll have to hide it when we stop for fuel along the way. I've had a special compartment built into the floor between the seats. It should fit there."

Diesel closed the door, waved at his teammates and fumbled trying to get the flight headset over his ears without contorting his sore arm.

Hands reached out from behind him and settled the headset over his ears. "How's that?" Reese asked.

He laid his hand over his shoulder to grasp hers. "Thanks." Once he was strapped in, he dismantled the rifle into two large pieces and stuffed them into his backpack. He then placed the backpack into the storage compartment between the seats.

Marly checked her instruments, started the

engine and the single propeller spun. "Hang on," she said into her mic, the sound carrying through to Diesel's ears.

He'd been up in so many different helicopters and large airplanes, but never a fixed-wing, small-bush plane. His gut knotted as the little craft bumped over the dirt landing strip, picking up speed with each passing second. At the end of the strip was the dense jungle. If they didn't lift off the ground soon, they'd plow right into the trees.

Diesel's fingers curled into fists. He couldn't close his eyes, even though his death appeared imminent.

Just when Diesel thought they couldn't possibly live through the takeoff, the little plane lifted off the ground, climbed into the air and barely missed the tops of the trees.

A chuckle filled his ears, and Marly shot an amused glance toward him. "Gives you a rush, doesn't it?"

"More like a heart attack," Reese said from the back seat, her voice shaking in Diesel's ear.

Marly laughed. "The runways in the jungle can be pretty short. Even I have to hold my breath and pray." She settled back with one hand on the yoke. "Might as well get comfortable. Next stop is Kananga to refuel."

Though he tried to stay awake during the flight, the hum of the motor lulled Diesel into sleep. Not until the engine slowed did he wake to find the plane descending into an airport with a flight tower and a couple of landing strips.

A small town was off to the side of the airport. On the road leading into the town, a plume of smoke rose from what appeared to be the hull of a vehicle.

Diesel leaned toward the window, his eyes narrowing. A truck loaded with men drove toward the airport. They appeared to be wearing green camouflage uniforms, and they carried weapons. From the distance, Diesel couldn't tell exactly what type of weapons, but he didn't have a good feeling about it.

"We might have some trouble here, but I don't have many choices on places I can land," Marly said. "We need fuel to continue on to Kinshasa. If you can, stay in the plane. If you have to make a trip inside to use the facilities, make it quick. The sooner we're back in the air, the better. The DRC military has had clashes with the Congolese rebels.

The battles can get bloody and neither side has much of a sense of humor these days."

"I hate to say it, but I need to use the facilities," Reese said from the seat behind them.

Marly nodded. "I do, too. We'll have to make it quick." She contacted the tower, received landing instructions and set the plane down on the runway, taxiing to the point at which she could purchase fuel.

Diesel was first to climb out, then Marly and finally Reese. While Marly negotiated for fuel, Diesel escorted Reese into the dingy terminal in search of a toilet.

Several people wearing brightly colored clothing waited inside with bags and boxes. When Reese and Diesel walked through the door, the people stopped talking and stared at them. Three men in Congolese military uniforms, carrying rifles, turned with narrowed gazes and watched as Reese walked across the floor toward what appeared to be a ladies' room.

Diesel needed to relieve himself, but he wouldn't until he knew Reese was okay. The bag of fluids Martha had given him had worked their way through his body. He waited outside the ladies' room for Reese to emerge, keeping an eye on the men with the weapons.

"Your turn," a voice said beside him. Reese smiled and tipped her head toward the room marked with a figure of a man.

"Are you sure you'll be okay?" he asked without shooting a glance in the direction of the men holding the rifles.

"I'll be fine. But you'd better hurry before that truckload of potential trouble arrives."

"On it." He entered the bathroom, relieved himself, washed up and was back out in less than two minutes.

The three armed men had left their position by the door and strode toward Reese.

She gave them a brief, but uninviting glance and turned toward Diesel with a huge smile. "There you are." Hooking her arm through his, she walked with him to the door leading out onto the tarmac, where the plane stood. "Isn't it a lovely day for flying?" she asked.

"You bet," he responded. And the sooner they were back in the air, the better. Out of the corner of his eye, he could see the truckload of Congolese soldiers nearing the airport.

Marly was overseeing a man who was

pumping fuel into the plane, when Reese and Diesel walked up to her.

"Watch him while I head inside. The fuel tank is almost full."

"The truckload of soldiers will be here within the next few minutes," Diesel warned.

"Then I'll make it fast." She jogged toward the terminal and disappeared inside.

The man pumping fuel into the little plane eyed them, but didn't say a word.

Diesel wished they could be in the plane and ready by the time Marly returned, but he wasn't sure he trusted the man fueling the plane. He kept an eye on the fueling process with glances toward the building the truck of soldiers had neared.

Moments later, Marly trotted out of the building, slowing her pace, probably so that she didn't appear anxious. She moved as fast as she could without raising too much suspicion. She shot a glance at the man who'd provided fuel and spoke to him in a language Diesel didn't understand. After a quick inspection of the exterior of the plane, she climbed inside.

Reese entered and took her seat. Diesel closed the door and took his seat beside the pilot.

He'd barely sat when Marly started the engine and contacted the tower. Moments later, Marly set the plane in motion, and the aircraft rolled down the runway.

They were just picking up speed, when suddenly several men carrying rifles burst through the doors of the terminal and ran out onto the tarmac.

"Come on, Betsy, pick up speed," Marly muttered, her words barely audible in the headset.

Diesel twisted in his seat, staring back over his shoulder at the men running for the runway. They aimed their weapons and fired.

"They're shooting at us!" Reese yelled.

Marly didn't slow the plane. She pushed the throttle as far forward as it would go, picking up speed. Then she pulled back on the yoke. The craft left the ground and climbed into the air.

Soon the Kananga airport was a speck in the distance.

Marly glanced at the array of instruments in front of her and sighed. "Doesn't look like they hit anything." She sat back and smiled. "Well, I bet you've never been on a vacation as exciting as this one, huh?"

Diesel shook his head. "I hope never to repeat it."

Marly pushed her sandy-blond hair back off her forehead. "You and me both." She grinned and shot a glance over her shoulder. "Next stop is Kinshasa."

Diesel remained awake and alert for the remainder of the journey to the capital city of the DRC. They didn't encounter any more difficulties or anything that would slow them.

Reese fell asleep in the back. She needed the sleep after her capture and subsequent escape into the harshness of the jungle.

Though Diesel's arm ached, it didn't feel as painful as it had before Martha and the doctor had worked on it. Hopefully he was well on his way to recovery. He couldn't afford to be down the use of one arm. Not when Reese still needed him to get her to the hotel where she would meet up with Klein.

Diesel leaned forward as they approached the Kinshasa International Airport.

The large, sprawling city of Kinshasa stood in stark contrast to the lush, green jungle surrounding the south and central areas of the Congo River.

The plane touched down on the runway and rolled to a stop in the general aviation area, away from the larger aircraft and the modern terminal.

"Thank you for delivering us safely." Diesel held out his hand.

Marly took it. "The pleasure was all mine. My usual route keeps me in Zambia, where it's not nearly as exciting."

"I could deal with a little less excitement," Reese said. "But right now, I'd settle for a shower and clean clothing."

"I hear you. I'm on my way back to Zambia. You two be safe." Marly shook Reese's hand and sat back, giving them the time and space they needed to get out.

Diesel grabbed his backpack from the compartment in the floor, exited the aircraft and held the door for Reese, helping her out onto the tarmac.

"Reese, darling, you don't know how happy I am to see you."

A man hurried forward, wearing a business suit, his neatly combed hair barely being ruffled by the wind.

Diesel stepped between the man and Reese. "Stop right there."

The man frowned, pulled himself up to his full height, which came to a few inches shorter than Diesel, and puffed out his chest.

"I'm Ferrence Klein. Miss Brantley works for me. Kindly step aside."

"I don't care who you are. Until I'm sure you're not carrying a weapon, you're not getting anywhere close to Miss Brantley."

"Seriously?" Klein's upper lip pulled back into a sneer. "You're standing in the way of work that must be done."

Diesel crossed his arms over his chest. "You're not getting past me until you empty your pockets and submit to a pat down."

The frown on Klein's face deepened. "Fine. Whatever it takes to see my employee." He opened his jacket, displaying the crisp white shirt beneath and no shoulder holster with a gun.

"Turn around," Diesel commanded.

"For the love of Mike." Klein turned.

"Spread your legs," Diesel said.

Klein did as asked. "Where did you find this goon, Reese?"

"In the jungle," Reese answered, a smile tugging the corners of her lips. "He's pretty determined. I suggest you do as he says."

Diesel patted the man's legs and hips, searching for weapons. When Klein came up clean, Diesel stepped back. "Miss Brantley has had a difficult few days. Don't delay her from the shower she so sorely deserves."

Klein glared at Diesel and stepped around him to face Reese. "What took you so long getting back? The Freedom and Human Rights Conference is tomorrow, and the ball is tomorrow night. I almost had to hire another assistant to attend with me."

Reese's eyes narrowed. "And who would that be?"

"How should I know? I couldn't go to the event without someone on my arm."

Diesel bit down hard on his tongue and clenched his fists, fighting the urge to smash Klein's face. What a jerk. The woman had been through hell and back in captivity and on the run through a hostile jungle. She was lucky to be alive. From what Reese had said, Klein didn't know she was more than an assistant.

"I need to get cleaned up. I don't suppose you had our luggage sent up from Zambia?"

"Thankfully, I had the good sense to have it flown to Kinshasa. All of my suits made it here undamaged."

Diesel's gaze met Reese's. She had to put up with the man as part of her job; otherwise, Diesel would have taken her hand and walked her away from the selfish bastard and seen to it she had what she needed.

"Did my luggage arrive with yours?" she asked, her tone even.

"Yes, yes, of course. Come on, the car is waiting." Klein sniffed. "Although, perhaps you should take a taxi. My dear, you smell awful."

Diesel hooked her arm. "She'll take a cab." And he'd be her escort all the way to the hotel.

Reese shook her arm free of Diesel's. "We'll take a taxi and follow you to the hotel. I can be cleaned up within an hour."

"Good, good." Klein walked ahead of them toward a gate leading off the flight line. "The sooner you're ready, the better. We have a social this evening with some of the members of the European and African Unions. I'll need you there with me to make notes about anything we need to follow up on." Klein kept talking all the way to the limousine he'd hired. Two guards stood on either side of the long white vehicle, each carrying a rifle and dressed in the military uniform of the Congolese Government.

"Did the Congolese president provide these men for you?" Reese asked.

Klein barely glanced at the men. "Yes, thankfully. There have been protests and run-ins with the rebels near the city. He's assigned guards to each of the diplomats attending the delegation."

"How close to the city have the outbursts been?" Reese asked.

"I don't know. Perhaps on the edge of the eastern suburbs. There was a scuffle in the downtown area last night, a few blocks from our hotel, but the military put a stop to it pretty quickly."

"What kind of scuffle?" Diesel asked. He didn't like what he was hearing. Kinshasa didn't sound much safer than the villages along the southeastern Congo River.

"Several thugs threw Molotov cocktails into a building."

The chauffeur opened the back door to the limousine.

Klein slid in. "I'll see you in two hours. Meet me at the bar in the hotel."

"Same hotel as on our original reservation?" Reese asked.

"Yes." Klein settled back in his seat. "Don't be late."

"Don't you want to wait and let us follow you to the hotel?" Reese asked.

"I have phone calls to make. If I wait for you to find a taxi, I might not have time to make those calls." The chauffeur closed the door, slid into the driver's seat and drove the limousine away.

Diesel shook his head, his gaze following the man in the fancy car. The two Congolese soldiers climbed into a camouflage SUV and followed. "That man is a piece of work."

"You're telling me." Reese sighed. "I can't protect him if he doesn't stay with me. I don't think he realizes that being in a city doesn't necessarily mean he's safe."

"I'd rather fight an army of ISIS than deal with political mumbo jumbo on a daily basis." He gripped her arm and started walking. "We can catch a cab in front of the airport terminal."

Now that they were in a civilized area, Reese was more aware of her dirty clothes, matted hair and filthy skin. She couldn't do anything about it until she got to the hotel. They walked to the terminal, found a cab and gave the driver the address of the hotel.

Diesel settled back against the seat, though his gaze scanned the roads and streets they passed, looking for any signs of trouble, his hand resting on his backpack.

Reese's lips quirked upward on the corners. She admired the man's dedication and complete awareness of his surroundings. He was smart, physically fit and determined to see her to her destination.

Kinshasa, home to over eleven million people, was perched on the southern side of the wide Congo River. High-rise buildings stretched toward the sky in the downtown area, and the slums spread south and east.

Traffic was slow as the taxi driver wove through the streets, dodging pedestrians, motorcycles and bicycles.

When the cab pulled up in front of the hotel, Reese's heartbeat kicked up several notches, and her chest tightened. Now that she had reached her destination, what would Diesel do? Would he hop back into the cab and return to the airport to catch the next flight out to Djibouti?

Though she'd only known him a couple days, Reese wasn't ready to part ways. They'd been through so much together. He'd helped her survive. *That counted for something.*

She stood in front of the hotel and realized she didn't have any money to pay the taxi driver. "I'll have to go find my luggage before I can pay him."

Diesel touched her dirty cheek and stared down into her eyes as though she weren't covered in jungle filth. "I've got this."

"But you shouldn't have to pay for my cab ride."

His lips curled upward, and his eyes twinkled. "I was in the cab with you."

"But you were escorting me."

He chuckled and tapped a finger to the tip of her nose. "Do you always argue this much? Oh, and you have a smudge on your cheek." With a wink, he turned to the cab driver and handed him a credit card. Once the transaction was completed, the cab driver left.

"You aren't headed straight for Djibouti?" she asked.

Diesel touched a hand to the small of her back and shook his head. "Nope. Not yet. I want to make sure you're safe."

"Hey, frogman," she whispered. "I've got news for you. *I'm* the bodyguard."

"To Klein. For now, I'm *your* bodyguard. Now hush and let's get you checked in and see if they have a spare room for me."

"You're staying?"

"I figure I have a couple days of leave I can use. And I'm not going anywhere until I get cleaned up." He wrinkled his nose. "I stink."

Reese didn't think so. The man smelled of the jungle and outdoors. Perhaps she smelled too much like him to know whether or not it smelled bad, but she didn't care. They were alive.

At the front desk, the clerk raised brows at their appearance, but went to work clicking the keyboard to find Reese's reservation. "Madame, you're lucky to arrive when you did," he said in a heavy French accent. "The hotel is completely booked, and if you had not come soon, we would have given your suite to someone on the standby list. Fortunately, your luggage was delivered this morning. Now, how many keys would you like?"

"The hotel is completely booked?" Reese asked.

"*Oui*," the clerk responded. "Many delegates from the European and African Unions, and others from all over the world, are here to attend the Freedom and Human Rights Convention. We've been booked for months." He ran a plastic key card. "One key or two?"

"Two, please," Reese responded.

Chapter Seven

Diesel's groin tightened. For a moment, he'd been considering where else he'd have to look for a hotel. In the next second, Reese had solved his problem and raised his body temperature.

The clerk nodded and ran another card through the machine. He handed both cards to Reese. "Enjoy your stay, madame, monsieur."

As they walked away, Diesel leaned close to Reese. "I can get a room somewhere else."

"Don't be silly. If they are full here, they'll be full all around here. Besides, I have a suite. You can clean up while you decide what you want to do next."

"Yes, ma'am." Diesel swallowed a chuckle, feeling lighter and happier than he had in days. Only steps away from a shower and walking beside the woman who'd been at his side for the past few days, things were really looking up.

With no luggage to carry to the room, and Diesel carrying his own backpack, they didn't need a bellman to show them the way.

The elevator took them to their floor, and moments later Reese pushed the door open to a beautiful, clean suite. She walked across the smooth white tile floor to the floor-to-ceiling windows at the far side of the sitting room, so that she could look out upon the Congo River. The sun was on its way toward the horizon, painting the sky in lovely shades of mauve, orange and purple.

"This high up, you can't really see the internal struggle of the people of the DRC," she said.

"No, but it's there. We experienced it," Diesel said, his attention captured by Reese, framed in one of the floor-to-ceiling windows, the sunset giving her a glow of faint pink and orange. Despite her disheveled appearance, the muted light managed to enhance her beauty and strength.

Reese nodded and glanced over her shoulder at him. "If you don't mind, I'll go first in the shower."

"That works. I'm going to duck out and

find some clean clothes." He had nothing but the outfit he'd worn to storm the kidnappers' camp.

Her eyes widened. "I'd completely forgotten you came without anything other than what you're wearing."

He shrugged. "No worries. I'll be back in less than an hour. Don't let anyone into this room until I return."

Her lips twisted. "Even my boss?"

Diesel snorted. "Especially your boss." He bent and brushed his lips across hers.

She stared up at him. "How can you do that?"

He lifted his head slightly, his gaze on the lips he wanted to take again. "Do what?"

"Kiss me when I'm so filthy?" she said, her voice airy, as if she couldn't quite catch her breath.

"In case you hadn't noticed, I'm just as dirty." He swept his thumb across her cheek. "I think you're beautiful."

She laughed shakily. "Seriously? What other drugs did Martha give you?" Reese shook her head. "Never mind. Go. Get some clothes and get back." Reese grabbed her suitcase and rolled it into the bedroom. "If you don't hurry, I'll use up all of the hot water."

"Going," he called out, on his way toward the exit. He paused with his hand on the doorknob and glanced back at Reese as she closed the door to the bedroom.

Everything had changed since they'd left the jungle. The city, the hotel, the modern conveniences were as different from the harshness of the jungle as night was from day. But his gut told him that it was no less dangerous. Yeah, they didn't have to worry about crocodiles so high up in the hotel, or gorillas climbing up to rip them apart. But the trouble in the Democratic Republic of the Congo was real.

Maybe he was being overly protective or paranoid, but Diesel couldn't leave Reese alone for long until that feeling went away. But if he was going to stay with her, he had to be dressed for the part. His combat clothes had to go.

REESE STARED AT the bedroom door, her heart suddenly racing. Her first inclination was to run after him and tell him to stay. Logic prevailed. The man was only going out to buy some clothes. He'd be back. What could happen to him in the city that was any worse than what had happened in the jungle? The man was a survivor.

Willing her pulse to slow back to normal, she dug through her case for toiletries, panties, a dress and shoes and carried them into the bathroom. After she peeled her torn, dirty clothes from her body, she shoved them into the wastebasket and turned to stare at herself in the mirror. Holy hell!

Dirty was putting it mildly. Her face was streaked with dirt and sweat, her hair looked like a rat's nest and she had bruises and cuts on just about every surface. She turned the shower on and stepped in, watching the clear water turn murky as the dirt mixed with the water and swirled down the drain.

Squeezing out a sizable glob of shampoo into her hand, she attacked her hair. Then with a fresh bar of soap, she went to work on scrubbing all of the jungle grime from her body. When she was done, she did it all again. Finally, the water running off her body was clear and clean.

Feeling like a completely different person, she turned off the water and stepped out onto the bath mat to dry off. Brushing the tangles out of her hair was harder than scrubbing the dirt off her body. She lost several clumps of hair to the bristles before she smoothed out every last knot. This time, when she glanced into the mirror, she almost recognized the woman staring back at her. Only, she was somewhat different. The time she had spent in the jungle with Diesel left her feeling strangely hopeful and optimistic about the future.

Whereas her captivity at the hands of the Taliban had left her very broken and angry, the time with Diesel had made her feel empowered and capable. Yes, he'd saved her life, but he'd appreciated the fact she could keep up with him. All the training she'd done to make her body strong and to be able to defend herself had paid off.

Being captured by the Congolese warlord had been nothing but bad luck. Had she not been thrown against the dash and knocked out, she could have forced the Zambian driver to stop before they drove across the border into the DRC.

She had managed to free Klein and escape captivity herself, before the SEALs showed up. They had helped to make good her escape, but she had no doubt she could have survived on her own.

But she was glad she'd had Diesel to help

get her out of the jungle. A shiver rippled down her spine in the air-conditioned room. On second thought, it had taken both of them to get through the jungle. Alone, she might have been the target of a hungry lion. And she never would have considered climbing a tree. No, Diesel had been the main reason she was standing in the hotel, fresh clean and alive.

Reese slipped into her bra, panties and the cocktail-length black dress she'd brought along for the social event that evening. When she stepped out of the bathroom, she glanced at the clock on the nightstand. She had exactly fifteen minutes before she was to meet Ferrence at the bar. Over an hour had passed since Diesel had left to find clothes.

She frowned at the door, willing it to open to the man she worried about. A nervous chuckle rose up her throat. Why she worried about Diesel, she didn't know. The man could clearly take care of himself.

Back in the bathroom, she brushed her teeth and then plugged in the blow-dryer and dried her clean hair. The long strands fanned out across her shoulders, the rich auburn tresses curling slightly at the ends. She wondered what Diesel would think of her hair now that it wasn't covered in dirt and dust. *Would he think it was pretty?*

Reese bent to place the blow-dryer beneath the cabinet and straightened to see another person in the mirror's reflection.

Diesel stood behind her, clean, freshly shaven and wearing a dark business suit, the white shirt beneath it making his tan seem even darker.

Reese's heart fluttered. The man was so handsome it almost hurt her eyes to look at him. "How?"

"The gym in the basement of the hotel had a shower. I knew if I showed up at a store to try on clothes, they'd run me off. So, I showered before I left." He held up his arm, displaying a price tag hanging from his sleeve. "They missed one."

Being so close to the man made her body temperature rise and heat rush into her cheeks. "I've got a pair of fingernail scissors in my bag," she said, her voice fading as her breath lodged in her lungs. He really was too handsome. He was causing her thoughts to scramble. "I'll just get it," she said, and started to brush past him.

His arm snaked out, blocking her path out

of the bathroom. "Wait. You have something on your chin."

Her eyes widened, and she raised her hand to her chin. "Where? Here?"

He took her hand and kissed the fingertips. "No. Here." Then he pulled her into his arms and kissed her chin, then migrated up to her lips.

Her hands rested against his chest, her fingers curling into the fabric of his new suit.

When he traced the seam of her lips with his tongue, she opened her mouth and let him in.

He claimed her in that kiss, crushing her body to his, sweeping her tongue in a long, sensuous caress.

Reese forgot everything outside the circle of his arms. Forgot she had a job to do. Forgot the past and all the horrors it held for her. In Diesel's arms, she was who she was meant to be and more. She slid her leg up the back of his calf, pressing her hips closer to his. How she wanted to shed her clothes and take him to her bed to make sweet love to him. Surely that was the reason they'd made it through the jungle and back to this hotel.

A knock on the door jolted her out of the fog of lust threatening to consume her.

She lifted her head and stared into Diesel's deep brown eyes. He had a speck of gold in one of them, making him even more attractive and a little mysterious.

Another knock sounded on the door. "Reese? Are you in there?" Ferrence's muffled voice sounded through the paneling, jerking Reese back to reality. "I have to go."

"I'm going with you," Diesel said, his tone firm.

She frowned. "I'm not sure I can get you in," she said. But she'd try. As long as he was still there, she wanted to be as close to him as possible. "Perhaps Mr. Klein can pull strings."

"Let's find out." Diesel brushed a kiss across her forehead. "You're beautiful."

She smiled, warmth spreading through her chest and everywhere else in her body. "You're not half-bad yourself."

He touched a strand of her hair. "I didn't know you were a redhead."

She laughed. "It was hard to tell with it being so dirty." Reese nodded toward the door. "We'd better go before Ferrence has housekeeping come unlock the door to check for dead bodies."

He glanced down at her feet and smiled. "I'll get the door, while you find some shoes."

Her cheeks heating and her core on fire, Reese hurried to the bedroom and slipped into the strappy silver stilettoes she'd chosen to go with the black dress. She prayed Ferrence could get Diesel into the social event, and maybe afterward, they'd come back to the suite and pick up where they'd left off on that kiss.

DIESEL BRACED HIMSELF against annoyance and opened the door to Ferrence Klein.

"Oh," the shorter man said and frowned. "I must have the wrong room."

"No, Mr. Klein, you have the correct room." Reese walked up, carrying a light silvery clutch in her hand. "We're ready to go, if you are."

"We?" He stared from Reese to Diesel and back. "I only have invitations for the two of us."

"Is there someone you can talk to about getting Mr. Landon in? I believe it would be worth a try. He's proven quite helpful in seeing to my safety. I'm sure he will be equally helpful in looking out for the both of us."

Klein's frown deepened. "I don't know. If

the dignitaries think I don't have confidence in their ability to see to my well-being, they might not want to negotiate with us."

"He could come as my fiancé," Reese said. "They don't have to know he's here to provide protection."

Diesel loved the irony of the situation. Klein didn't know Reese was there to provide for his protection, and here she was volunteering Diesel to be their backup, as long as their hosts didn't catch wind.

The diplomat's face hardened. "I had hoped to have you acting as my date."

Reese crossed her arms over her chest. "Considering your wife is at home with your children, perhaps it would be better if my fiancé tags along, don't you think?"

Diesel almost raised his hand to give Reese a high-five, but he restrained himself and let her manage her boss. Knowing her, she wouldn't appreciate him butting in or punching the man in the face, as he sorely wished he could.

"Well, I suppose you're right. But I need you to be with me at all times in case I miss something. You are my assistant, after all."

Reese nodded. "Yes, I am. And I'll be with you throughout the evening."

"Well, then, let's get this over with. We'll make an appearance, talk with the president and call it a night. The convention starts tomorrow. It'll be a long day of meetings."

Reese followed Klein out of the suite and to the elevator.

Diesel was glad he'd gone to the trouble of getting the suit. Had he not, he'd be waiting in the suite, cooling his heels while Reese was off with the lecherous Ferrence Klein.

He clenched his fists and reminded himself that Reese was perfectly capable of handling her boss. It was the rest of the delegates he should be concerned about. Some of the countries represented at the convention had little to no respect for women, their rights or their safety.

The elevator took them to the second floor, where half of the ballroom had been sectioned off to provide a more intimate space for the smaller social gathering of a few chosen dignitaries.

Diesel didn't recognize any of them. Most wore expensive, tailored suits or long, elaborate robes, depending on their faith or the country they represented. Although there were some women in the room, the preponderance of people there were men. And they appeared to be businessmen, many of them white.

"I thought this was supposed to be a summit of the African Union," he said.

"This social is for the businessmen who have interest in the DRC. They want to make sure their interests are being represented in these meetings," Klein said. "There's the president. I want to speak with him before the room gets too full." Klein hurried across the room with Reese at his side.

Diesel followed at a slower pace, taking in all the guests and the military men dressed in neatly pressed uniforms, but still carrying their rifles. He didn't like that he'd had to hide his own rifle in the suite, still stashed in his backpack.

If one of the military guards started shooting, it would be a massacre in a matter of seconds. A chill rippled across the back of Diesel's neck. The ball would be held in the same place the next night. He wondered if they would have the same military presence stationed throughout the room. He also wondered if the exterior of the building was being guarded as well.

Diesel hurried to catch up to Klein and Reese. Perhaps he'd been involved in too many skirmishes. He thought too much about different scenarios. With as many dignitaries in town, the president of the Democratic Republic of the Congo would have heightened security, especially since there were rebel factions stirring up trouble in the country, based on what Klein had told them.

Diesel had read about the president of the DRC and how he was known to be heavy-handed with his use of military force. Though the president was an elected position, the current one wasn't keen on giving up the job. He'd delayed the elections, claiming the country was not stable enough to hold them when they were supposed to be held. The truth was he didn't want to be voted out of office.

And he was the host of this event. He had a lot riding on his ability to maintain the peace and keep the dignitaries safe while they were in Kinshasa.

As Klein and Reese reached the president, a scuffle broke out behind Diesel. He turned to see the guards holding a man at the door. The man appeared dressed in a ceremonial uniform and headdress. He struggled against the guards holding him back from entering the room.

He shouted something across the room toward the location where Reese and Klein were standing.

Diesel couldn't understand his words, as they were spoken in one of the languages indigenous to the Congo.

The president's chin lifted, and he answered in French, the official language of the DRC.

Diesel had taken French in high school, but he could only pick up on a few words. One of them being *brother* and the other being *go*.

He knew the president of the DRC had a brother who'd planned to run in the next election. It appeared the brother hadn't been invited to the social and was attempting to crash the party.

The president excused himself from the people gathered around him and walked across the floor and out the door with his brother.

Diesel joined Reese and Klein.

"Well, that wasn't helpful," Ferrence complained. "I wanted to speak with the president since I couldn't get a meeting alone with him while I'm here."

"Why are you so intent on meeting with the president?" Diesel asked.

"The mines in the Congo are rich with minerals everyone in the world wants," Ferrence said, his voice hushed in the crowded room. "We need to make sure we have a stake in the mining industry. The Russians and Chinese have been funding development of the mining operations. We can't let them take everything. We need the copper, gold and other minerals for our own country's needs."

Diesel watched the door, waiting for the president's return. "And what does that have to do with the US?"

"We suspect President Jean-Paul Sabando sold half the interest in one of the major copper mines to an undisclosed party," Reese continued. "Ferrence is here to find out if he sold it and to whom."

"And if he did, then what?" Diesel asked.

"We attempt to find out who has it and try to purchase it from them."

"Since when does the US negotiate purchases of mine interests with foreign countries?"

"Since we need those minerals in the production of our weapons," Klein said. "And the US won't be the ones to purchase the interest. It would be one of our primes who provide the materials we need for weapons production."

"The president's brother, Lawrence Sabando, is running on the platform of returning the profits to the people of the DRC," Klein said. "Rumor has it he's got the backing of Bosco Mutombo, one of the major warlords responsible for attacks on the mine."

"Bosco Mutombo?" Reese frowned. "I could swear he was in charge of the men who abducted us."

Klein's brows drew together. "In which case, we're lucky to be here."

Reese's lips thinned. "Luck had nothing to do with it. Diesel and his men got us out of there."

Klein nodded. "Yes, yes, of course."

"And Lawrence decided it was a good idea to crash his brother's party?" Diesel shook his head. "Sounds like a recipe for trouble."

Klein craned his neck to see over the crowd, watching the entrance for the president's return. "Like I said, there was an incident involving Molotov cocktails last night at a building not far from here."

"What building?" Reese asked.

"The headquarters of Metro Mining Company, one of the state-owned mining companies of the DRC," Klein said. "They are responsible for the mining of the copper mine the president sold half interest in."

Diesel shook his head. "Are you sure it's a good idea to be in the DRC right now?"

"I'm here on my father's behalf to establish a conversation with the president." Klein lifted his chin. "My father would be here, but he's tied up with the troubles in Libya. The US president wanted him in Washington if anything broke out."

"So you're here, in a hostile environment and have already been kidnapped once by Congolese rebels and held for ransom." Diesel didn't like it. "Why?"

"From what my father told me, they were demanding a lot of money. Money the US government could have handed over to free me. I suspect they wanted the money to fund their supplies to keep up the fight." Klein stood straighter. "As far as President Sabando is concerned, I was never kidnapped or held for ransom. My father didn't want to give the rebels any more credit than we can help."

"Okay," Diesel said, "But what's to keep the rebels from making another attempt on your life, or one of the other delegates here for the convention?"

"I'm glad you asked." Klein gave him a hint of a smile. "Since you insisted on coming to this social, it's given me an idea. I'll work with my father to see if we can get more help here to protect the people at the convention. Of course, whoever helps would have to be undercover. We couldn't let Sabando catch wind we don't trust his security forces. I bet my father could get the team that rescued me to provide the support we need for tomorrow."

"Only if we get on the phone now. It takes time to get them from where they are to Kinshasa, and they'll need appropriate attire for the mission. Combat gear would be a dead giveaway." Diesel's brows pulled together as he worked through the logistics in his head.

"I'll see what I can do to make it happen." Klein pulled out a shiny new cell phone and walked off to a deserted corner of the ballroom to place his call.

Reese and Diesel followed, but stood far enough away to give the man privacy for his call.

"Do you think your team could be here and in place by tomorrow?" Reese asked.

"You'd be surprised how fast they can deploy. And since they're already on this continent, they could be here by morning."

Klein rejoined them, his lips forming a thin line. "It's done. Your team should be receiving orders within the hour."

Chapter Eight

Reese was beginning to think they'd bit off more than they could chew in the DRC. With warring factions pushing the limits and warlords looking for ways to fund their war machines, Ferrence Klein, the son of the US Secretary of Defense, was a prime target.

Her experience as both a soldier and an MMA fighter would be precious little protection if they were cornered again by Congolese rebels.

President Sabando didn't return to the social event. After waiting for him for the next hour following his departure, Klein called it a night.

Fortunately, he and Reese had rooms on the same floor. His room directly across the hallway from Reese's made it possible for her to hear if he was being attacked. On the other hand, he was right across the hall from her.

Which meant little privacy. The three of them rode the elevator up to their floor. When they reached Klein's door, Diesel asked for his key.

Klein frowned. "Why?"

"Let me make sure your room hasn't been compromised. Anyone of the maintenance staff could let himself in. And they could have been bribed to let someone else in."

Klein handed over his key and waited in the hallway with Reese as Diesel searched his room for intruders or booby traps.

When he emerged, he handed the key to Klein. "I'll be across the hall if you should need me. Lock the dead bolt and don't answer the door unless it's one of us."

"I arrived before you two," Klein said. "You'd think if anyone was going to do something, they already would have."

"Except Diesel's team got you out of the jungle with the express purpose of keeping your rescue on the down low," Reese reminded him. "If the same folks who ordered the kidnapping were going to sabotage your room, they wouldn't have known you'd show up when you did. They might still have been under the impression you were secured in the jungle somewhere."

"No one was expecting you to arrive," Diesel said. "Now that you've shown your face at a gathering, they'll know you escaped. You're back to being a target."

"Great." Klein shook his head. "I guess I'll be sleeping with one eye open tonight."

"Again, we're across the hallway."

"Why not stay in my suite?" Klein suggested.

Reese held her breath. It made sense to have Diesel stay with the Secretary of Defense's son. But she didn't want him to. She wanted him in her room, doing what he'd done earlier, and more.

Diesel shook his head. "We set the precedent. I'm here as Miss Brantley's fiancé. If you suspect someone is trying to break in, and you think I won't hear it, you can call. I'll be there."

Klein nodded. "Okay, then. I'll see you two in the morning." His eyes narrowed. "Don't do anything I wouldn't do."

Reese refused to rise to his taunt and smiled as the man closed the door. "Which means the sky's the limit," she muttered and turned with her key to open the door to her suite.

As soon as she crossed the threshold, butterflies erupted in her belly, and her body tingled all over. She was alone with Diesel, and they weren't being shot at or threatened by a troop of gorillas. The possibilities exploded in her head, and her core heated.

She didn't turn around, afraid Diesel would see the desire in her eyes. *What if he wasn't feeling it as deeply as she was?*

She heard the door close behind her and felt a hand catch hold of hers, spinning her around.

"Come here," he said, his voice low, throaty and sexy as hell, melting every bone in her body. *How did he do that?*

Reese hadn't been with a man in so long… She tried not to think about the last time. She'd been raped by Taliban fighters. As far as she was concerned, it didn't count. She pushed the memories to the back of her mind and concentrated on the real electricity firing off all of her nerve synapses, sending fire to her center.

And took back ownership of her body.

Since her abuse at the hands of the Taliban, she'd thought she wasn't capable of feeling the intensity of lust and desire. "I was wrong. So very wrong," she whispered.

His head dipping low, Diesel stopped before his lips reached hers. "Wrong?" He leaned back and stared into her eyes, his brows knitting. "Did I read you wrong? Are you not feeling what I'm feeling?"

She laughed and wrapped her hands around the back of his head and pulled him down for a quick kiss, before saying, "No. I was wrong. I thought I would never feel what I'm feeling now."

"And what are you feeling?" he asked, tucking a strand of her hair behind her ear.

She drew in a deep breath and let it out. She told herself that he wouldn't be holding her like he was if he didn't feel the same. "Every cell in my body is on fire."

"I hope in a good way." He brushed his lips across her forehead.

"Only the best." She smiled up at him, but the smile faded. "You need to know something, though."

"Shoot. After our trek through the jungle, and facing the wrath of a giant gorilla, I think I can handle just about anything."

Reese dipped her head and stared at the tips of her toes in the stilettoes. "I haven't had sex with anyone since I was a Taliban captive."

Diesel drew in a deep breath and let it out

slowly. Then he gathered her in his arms and held her, stroking the back of her head, his lips pressed to her temple. "Sweetheart, if I could, I'd kill every one of those bastards."

"You and me both." She laid her cheek against his chest and listened to the beat of his heart. "When I was liberated, the army ran me through all the tests for STDs. I'm clean, but because of how rough they treated me, I'm damaged. Remember, I told you before, I'll never have children."

"Oh, Reese, darlin', you're not damaged. You're perfect. Don't let anyone tell you differently." He tilted her chin up and stared into her eyes. "You're strong, brave and you have a big heart." He smiled down at her. "In my eyes, that's perfect."

"I always felt dirty after that." Her eyes filled with tears, but she managed to grin. "Until I showered earlier, I hadn't realized how much cleaner I've felt since I met you. Inside and out. And you're making me feel things I never thought I would feel ever again."

"Like you're on fire?"

She nodded. "Like a flame is burning inside, making my blood warm and my heart beat faster. Please tell me I'm not silly. Am I the only person who has ever felt like this?"

"No, you're not." He threaded his fingers through her hair and brushed his lips across hers. "I'm feeling it, too. It's like electricity is humming through my body, and it's all because of you. I can't seem to get close enough to you."

Reese knew exactly what he meant. Their bodies touched from their lips to their thighs but it wasn't enough. She wanted to be closer.

But first…the kiss.

He claimed her mouth, thrusting his tongue between her teeth to sweep alongside hers, caressing it in long, slow swirls.

Reese gave as good as she got, wrapping her hands behind his head, threading her fingers through his short hair. The longer the kiss went on, the weaker her knees became. She wrapped a leg around his, rubbing her aching center against his thick, muscular thigh. She wanted him inside her, filling the emptiness that had been with her since she'd left the military.

When Diesel broke the seal of their kiss, he pressed his forehead to hers.

Reese dragged in breaths, filling her lungs. Her heart raced and her knees wobbled. This man had such a profound effect on her, she couldn't control her reaction. Before she could think or talk herself out of it, she pushed his jacket off his shoulders. By the time the garment hit the floor, her hands had moved to the buttons on his shirt, sliding them through the holes, her fingers shaking, eager, desperate to reach the skin beneath.

When one button got stuck, she tore at it.

"Hey." He chuckled and laid a hand over hers. "I need this shirt for tomorrow."

"Sorry. It's just...you have on too many clothes." She glanced up at his face, her brows drawing together. "Are you just going to stand there and make me do all the work?" She brushed his hand aside and attacked the button again. "I can't get you naked fast enough," she muttered beneath her breath.

"Sweetheart, we have all night." He pushed her hand aside and deftly flicked the button through the hole. He repeated the action with the next three buttons, his motion pulling the shirttail out of the waistband of his trousers.

Reese was already working on the button on his trousers. She then proceeded to slide the zipper down.

His shaft jutted out of the opening into her

palm, and she looked up, giving him what had to be a goofy smile. "Commando?"

"Always," he said.

"I should have guessed." She wrapped her hand around his length and tried to remember to breathe. This was what she wanted, him naked, inside her, thrusting, filling, becoming a part of her. She hooked her thumbs in the waistband of his trousers and shoved them down his legs. God, she hoped she didn't freeze at the wrong moment. Deep inside, she knew she was ready, but that PTSD stuff had a bad habit of debilitating her when she least expected. A sexual situation would be the most likely to trigger her into a downward spiral.

Diesel toed off his shoes, bent to remove his socks and stood in front of her completely naked. He was the most beautiful man she'd ever seen.

He arched his brows. "You're overdressed for the occasion."

Trying not to salivate, Reese turned her back to him, her entire body shaking.

His fingers curled around her shoulders, and he pulled her back against his front, his staff pressing against her bottom. "Tell me if I move too fast. Just say *no*, and I'll stop."

"Are you kidding me?" She laughed shakily. "I just stripped the clothes off your body. Does that say *no* to you?" Dear sweet heaven she wanted him, and he was taking far too long to get her naked.

His hands slid downward, gripped the zip on the back of her dress and lowered it to the base of her spine. She tilted her head back, letting her hair brush across her back, liking the way it felt.

Then he skimmed her shoulder blades with his fingertips and slipped them beneath the straps, inching them over her shoulders. The little black dress slid down to pool at her hips.

Diesel leaned over and kissed the curve of her neck, pushing her hair aside to nibble on her earlobe.

Reese shivered and leaned her head to the side, giving him full access to her neck. He accepted the invitation and laid a trail of kisses along the length and back to the curve of her shoulder. Meanwhile his fingers lowered to the clasp of her bra, and he unhooked it.

Tied in knots and eager to get the show on the road, Reese shrugged out of the bra and let it slide down her arms to the floor. Then she raised her hands to the dress gathered around her waist.

Diesel beat her to it and pushed the dress over the swell of her bottom, slowly, letting his hands ride down her hips until the dress slipped to the floor in a puddle of black fabric.

He hooked his thumbs into the elastic of her panties and dragged them down her legs, going down on one knee to reach her ankles.

When she stepped out of them, she started to reach for the clasp on her shoes.

"Don't," he said and pressed a kiss to one of her lower cheeks, and then the other. Rising, as if in slow motion, he kissed the small of her back and dragged his hands up her thighs to rest on her hips.

His shaft pressed against her bottom, hard, thick and hot.

"I can't wait any longer," she whispered, her core so hot, she feared she'd spontaneously combust before they actually made it to the bed.

"Me either." Then he scooped her up into his arms and carried her into the bedroom.

This was it, this would be her first time since…

And her only thought was if it felt this

good now, it could only be better when he finally came inside her.

DIESEL LAID HER on the edge of the bed, parted her knees and hooked his arms beneath her thighs. He wanted to thrust into her, hard, fast and all the way to the hilt. But this woman had suffered at the hands of their enemy. A horrible, tragic abuse of her body. She needed to know it didn't have to be that way. He wanted her to know and feel how good making love was when the person doing it cared.

Drawing in a deep breath, he released her thighs and bent over her to kiss her lips, long, slow and gentle. He'd bring her to the brink, to that pinnacle of desire before he slaked his own.

Reese wrapped her arms around his neck, arched her back and pressed her breasts to his chest.

She was going to make it hard for him to hold back.

He unwound her arms from around his neck and pressed her back against the mattress. "Let me show you how good it can be."

"Just don't take forever. I'm really a quick

learner, and I want you. What more do we need?" she said, her voice quivering.

"If you have to ask, you don't know." Then he kissed a path across her cheek and down the side of her neck. He didn't stop until he brushed his lips over the swell of her breast, taking the nipple into his mouth. He tongued the tip until it formed a hard, little bead that he then rolled between his teeth.

Reese moaned. She cupped the back of his head and guided him to the other breast, where he then performed the same treatment. When he had her squirming beneath him, he moved down her torso, flicking his tongue across her skin, dipping into her belly button and then moving lower to the tuft of hair at the juncture of her thighs.

Her body stiffened.

"Are you afraid I won't stop?" he asked and blew a stream of air across the curls.

"No, I'm afraid you *will* stop. Please, don't." She widened her thighs, giving him better access to his goal. He dropped to his knees and looped her legs over his shoulders. Then he parted her folds with his thumbs and touched the strip of nerve-packed flesh at her center with the tip of his tongue.

She gasped and arched her back off the bed. "Oh, please."

He chuckled. "Please, what?"

"Do it again."

"As you wish," he said, breathing warm air over her heated flesh. He flicked her again, this time staying long enough to swirl his tongue the length of the nubbin, drawing from her a long, low moan.

He swirled and pressed a finger to her entrance, pleased by how damp and ready she was. Still licking and flicking, he slid a finger inside her channel.

Reese bucked off the mattress and laid a hand over his.

He froze, afraid he'd scared her.

When she curled her fingers around his hand and urged him deeper, he wanted to yell *hallelujah*. He sent another finger into her and then another, stretching her and pumping in and out to prepare her for when he came to her.

Her juices drenched his fingers, making him so hard, he couldn't hold out much longer. He flicked and swirled until she raised her feet, still wearing the shoes, and dug them into the mattress. Sweet heaven, she was sexy, pushing her hips up as her body pulsed and trembled with her release.

Diesel didn't stop what he was doing until her bottom lowered to the bed. Then he pushed to his feet, reached into the nightstand for the accordion of condom packages he'd stashed there earlier when Reese had been in the bathroom. He tore one off, opened it and rolled it down over his throbbing shaft.

Then he hooked her knees in his arms and pulled her bottom to the edge of the bed, nudging her soft, wet entrance with his hardness. "Are you okay with this? I can stop now."

"Oh, please, whatever you do, don't stop now." She wrapped her legs around his waist and pulled him into her.

He entered her slowly, giving her body a chance to adjust to his length and girth. When he'd sunk all the way to the hilt, he stopped, breathing in and out, afraid he'd scare her if he went too fast.

"Faster," she said on a gasp. "Faster and harder. I want to feel every bit of you."

He obeyed, sliding out and then back in, increasing the pressure and the force with every thrust.

Reese flung back her head and arched off the bed, tightening her thighs to bring him deeper.

He pumped in and out of her until his body tensed and heat radiated from his center, sending electric tingles out to the very tips of his fingers and toes. Diesel thrust into her one last time and held her tightly against him, his shaft throbbing inside. His heart was pounding so hard in his chest, he thought it might break his ribs.

When he finally came back to earth, he gathered Reese in his arms and scooted her up onto the bed, laying her head on a pillow. Then he dropped down beside her, spooned her body from behind and cupped a breast. He kissed the curve of her shoulder. "Are you okay?"

"I don't think I'll ever be okay again," she said, her voice sexy and gravelly. She wiggled her body against his. "I'll forever be fabulous. *Okay* is for underachievers." She laid a leg over his and wrapped his arms around her. "Thank you."

Diesel chuckled.

"What?" She turned her head in an attempt to look at his face.

"Nothing. You just make me happy." He

pulled her closer, kissed her temple and reflected on how incredibly lucky he'd been to find her in the jungle.

His life couldn't be better than at that moment. Tomorrow they'd have to sort through what had just happened, but tonight was everything he could have dreamed of.

"Diesel?" Reese said, her voice barely above a whisper.

"Yeah, babe?" He brushed her hair aside and kissed her shoulder.

"Do you really think Sabando's brother will try something stupid while the delegates are attending the conference?"

"I don't know. But there are a lot of important people here from all over the world. If his brother is desperate enough, he might."

Reese lay quietly for several minutes.

Diesel thought she'd gone to sleep.

"Diesel?"

"Yeah, babe?"

"Do you think your team will get here in time?"

He chuckled. "You bet. It might be overkill to bring them here, but I'd rather have overkill and nothing happen than do nothing and innocent people die."

Silence settled in around them. Sleep was just a blink away.

"Diesel?"

"Mmm?"

Reese yawned and stretched her lithe, sexy body against his. When she settled back into him, she sighed. "What's going to happen tomorrow?"

"At the conference? I have no clue."

"No," she whispered. "Between us?"

"I don't know, but we'll figure out something."

She hugged his arm around her and pressed it to her breasts.

Diesel's body jerked awake, his groin tightening at her touch. He willed his desire to recede.

Reese needed her sleep, and so did he. Tomorrow might be more of an event than even the attendees anticipated. At least his team would be there to provide backup.

Chapter Nine

A firm knock on the door in the outer room of the suite broke through the dead of sleep Reese had fallen into. For a moment, she lay comfortable, surrounded by the luxury of clean sheets and an incredibly soft mattress. She didn't want to wake up, but the incessant knocking forced her to open her eyes.

Diesel was already out of the bed, running for the other room, stark naked. Through the open bedroom door, Reese could see him snatch up his suit trousers from the floor where he'd left them and jam his legs into them. Half running, half hopping, he made it to the door on the third round of knocking. A quick peek through the peephole, and he flung the door wide.

"Damn, you guys got here fast," he said quietly and opened the door wide, grinning.

Five hulking men, dressed in dark pants

and T-shirts stretched tightly over broad chests and massive biceps, tumbled into the room.

Reese yelped, rolled out of the bed and dropped to floor on the other side, where she'd laid her suitcase. She dug through, searching for her workout clothes and sports bra. While lying on the floor, she dressed quickly, her heart pounding, and her cheeks on fire.

When she was convinced all pertinent parts were covered, she straightened, pretending that getting up off the floor of a hotel room was a natural occurrence. She could have been exercising for all they knew.

And pigs might learn to fly.

Diesel's men would all know she'd been in bed with their teammate as soon as they caught sight of the discarded clothing on the sitting-room floor.

The man she'd made love with stood in the middle of the group of men, each back-slapping and filling each other in on the other's stories.

Reese stepped into the room and cleared her throat.

Diesel turned, grinned and held out his hand for her.

She took his and allowed him to draw her into the circle of his friends.

"Guys, you remember Reese Brantley. Reese, this is just part of my team. Apparently, they only got clearance to send them, no more. Which is probably for the better. Too many SEALs in a public place would raise red flags all over the world."

Reese remembered most of their faces from the boat ride the day before. "Hi. I'm sorry, I don't remember your names."

Diesel pointed to a man about the same height as him with black hair and brown eyes. "This is Harmone Payne."

He held out his hand. "Harm."

"I don't understand." Reese took his hand, a frown drawing her brows together. "I have no intention of harming you."

Harm laughed. "The team calls me *Harm*."

Heat climbed into her cheeks. "Oh. Sorry. Harm, it is."

"You remember me, Graham Buckner." A brown-haired man with bright blue eyes held out his hand. "You can call me Buck."

"Percy Taylor." Another hand was shoved toward her by a man with short dark hair and hazel eyes. He was stockier than the others and built like a freight train. "But you might remember me as Pitbull."

"On account he looks like one," Diesel said.

"And smells like one," Buck added.

Pitbull swung a fist at Buck, hitting him hard in the shoulder.

Reese flinched, imagining the pain of that meaty fist on her own shoulder. But Buck didn't seem to notice.

"I'm Trace McGuire." A man with dark auburn hair and blue eyes held out his hand.

Buck leaned close. "That's T-Mac to most."

The biggest man in the room stepped forward. Reese remembered him. "Jake Schuler." He had dark blond hair and gray eyes. He tipped his head toward his buddies. "You'll remember me as the one called Big Jake."

Reese smiled at the men. Even at five-foot-eight, she felt dwarfed by their size and extra-large, alpha-male personalities. "Have you been up all night?" she asked.

"We have," Big Jake said. "We could use some shut-eye, but the front desk said the hotel was full. We thought we'd let you know we were here before we looked for other accommodations."

Diesel shook his head. "You aren't likely to find anything nearby. Not with the convention in town."

Buck glanced around the suite. "There's enough room here. We could catch a few Z's."

The corners of Reese's mouth quirked upward. "On the floor?"

"Lady, we've slept on worse," Buck admitted. "The floor would be heaven."

Harm nodded. "We only need a couple hours to recharge our batteries."

"Do you mind?" T-Mac asked.

Reese laughed and frowned. "Not at all. Are you sure you'll be all right on the floor?"

"Perfectly," Big Jake yawned. "I could sleep on a bag of rocks about now."

"Hopefully it won't be that bad." Reese hurried for the bedroom. "I'll get some pillows and whatever blankets I can find. But you might want to keep it down. The hotel staff will kick us all out if they find out I've got six men in my room."

Diesel grabbed their clothes from where they'd landed on the floor and tossed them on the bed. Then he helped her gather the spare blankets and pillows from the closet, and a couple from the bed, and carried them out to the five men stripping out of their shirts and boots.

Reese's eyes widened at all of the muscles on display. She was in every woman's paradise.

Diesel nudged her with his elbow. "Hey, don't get any ideas. I'd like to think you're all mine."

She smothered a giggle. "You can't blame me. It's like looking at works of art." Reese dropped the pillows and blankets on the sofa. "I believe that sofa folds out into a bed."

"I call it," T-Mac said.

"Sorry, dude. I'm pulling rank on this one." Big Jake nudged the auburn-haired SEAL out of the way. "You can have the cushions."

"Deal. Actually, that sounds better anyway." T-Mac gathered the cushions from the sofa and carried them to a corner of the sitting room.

Pitbull snagged a pillow and stretched out in front of the floor-to-ceiling window. He didn't ask for a blanket or a spare sheet. He lay down and closed his eyes. Within seconds, his chest began to rise and fall in deep, restful breaths.

Harm draped his body over a large chair and was snoring within seconds.

Buck grabbed a pillow. "Do we need someone to stand watch?"

"Not tonight," Diesel said. "We'll come up with a plan in the morning. I'm not sure I can get all of you into the convention center. But having you close by will be a relief."

Buck nodded to Diesel and Reese. "Okay, then. I'm catching a few Z's. See you two when the sun comes up." The big man found an empty space near the door.

Big Jake unfolded the bed from inside the sleeper sofa and dropped onto the thin mattress. He gave Diesel a salute, crossed his arms over his chest and closed his eyes.

Diesel clasped Reese's hand in his and led her back to the bedroom and closed the door.

"How do they do that?" Reese asked, amazed at how quickly they settled in for sleep.

"Do what?"

She shook her head. "Go to sleep so fast?"

"Part of it is that they're tired. That, and they're used to grabbing a nap whenever and wherever they can. You never know when you'll get to sleep again."

Reese nodded. "Like when we were in the jungle."

"Exactly." He pulled her into his arms and

kissed her soundly. "As much as I'd like to make love to you again, we should get some sleep, as well."

"Yeah, you two need to sleep," Buck called out from the other side of the door. "We don't need reminders of how lonely we are out here."

"Speak for yourself, dirtbag. You can always snuggle up to me," T-Mac said.

"In your dreams," Buck shot back.

Reese's face heated, but she chuckled. "Sleep it is." She could have gone for another round of lovemaking with her handsome SEAL but not with an audience of five of his buddies on the other side of what appeared to be a paper-thin bedroom door.

Diesel stroked his thumb along the side of her cheek. "Do you want me to sleep out there with the guys?"

She frowned. "Hell, no."

"Does it bother you that they know we're sleeping together?"

Reese stood on her toes and pressed a kiss to his lips. "I'm a grown woman. What I do and who I sleep with is my business, and I don't give a damn what anyone else thinks."

"You tell him, Reese," Buck said.

Diesel growled. "Go to sleep, Buck."

"I would, if you two would stop yammering," Buck grumbled.

Reese took Diesel's hand and led him to the bed. She lay down, fully dressed in her workout clothes.

Diesel stripped out of his trousers and slipped beneath the sheets, pulling her body against his.

She touched a finger to his chest. "I want to get closer, but—"

"Shh. There are far too many men in this suite. Go to sleep knowing that at least you're safe."

She pressed her ear to his skin, listening to the strong, steady beat of his heart, her own swelling inside. This was a man worth keeping. Someone she could easily fall for. Too bad they were in such difficult jobs. They'd never find time to be together. She'd have to settle for what little time they had together for the next couple days. Her memories would have to carry her for a long time. Finding someone like Diesel would be impossible. He'd set the bar for her. No one else would ever do. Eventually, exhaustion claimed her, and Reese slipped into a troubled sleep.

DIESEL LAY FOR a long time, wishing the guys hadn't come as soon as they had, but glad they were there.

He wanted to make love to Reese again, but the others would hear and give him and her hell. Until they made it through the conference and got Reese and Klein on their way back to the States, he would just have to abstain. But it was hard. Really hard.

When he finally went to sleep, it felt like only moments before an alarm blared on the nightstand nearby.

Reese reached out and turned it off, and then rolled over into his arms and kissed him. "They can't hear if I kiss you," she whispered, and did it again.

Diesel gathered her close and took her mouth, thrusting his tongue past her teeth to spar with hers. He could get used to waking up every day to this strong, beautiful woman.

But he was a SEAL. He would always be on call and deploy at the drop of a hat. He'd seen too many SEALs divorce within the first few years of marriage. Their wives couldn't stand the uncertainty, never knowing when they would be home, or if they would arrive in a body bag.

Reese deserved better. After what she'd been through at the hands of the Taliban terrorists, she deserved someone who could be there to protect her every day, not just a part-time lover who would enter and leave her life at the whim of the navy.

He kissed her hard, wishing they could stay in bed for the entire day, but knowing they had a job to do. He smacked her bottom. "You can have the bathroom first. I want to work with the guys to come up with a plan."

"I want to be in on the planning, too," she insisted.

"Then you better hurry. Your boss's meetings begin in less than an hour, and my guys will want to grab something to eat before the fun begins."

"Going," she said, grabbed his ears and pulled him to her again for another kiss. Then she scrambled from the bed and raced to the bathroom.

Diesel pulled on his suit trousers and walked out of the bedroom.

T-Mac crouched by the window, unpacking items from a duffel bag, laying them out on the floor.

Harm was checking out the coffee maker.

"One lousy cup. Why bother?" He glanced up as Diesel entered the room. "We have to make a run for coffee."

"We will, after we discuss the mission." Big Jake pulled a polo shirt over his head and tucked it into his khaki pants. "What are the chances of us getting into the conference?"

"I'd say slim to none," Diesel replied. "From what I've seen so far, only the attendees will be allowed into the auditorium. I assume they'll have tight security around the conference center."

"We had orders to come provide any help we can," Big Jake said.

"But we aren't supposed to be here, so we weren't allowed to carry weapons," Harm added.

"What good can we be without firepower?" Pitbull asked.

"You can let us know if you see, hear or smell trouble," Diesel said.

"That means we'll be the eyes, ears and noses." Buck lightly backhanded Diesel in the belly as he passed him and bent to the equipment T-Mac was laying out on the floor. "I'll take one of those."

"I figured you might have lost yours in

your run through the jungle." T-Mac handed Diesel one of the tiny radio headsets that fit in the ear and that would pick up the sound of his voice, providing two-way communication.

"Great. Did you bring an extra for Reese?" Diesel asked. "I probably won't be allowed into the conference center with her and Klein, but I'd like to keep in contact."

"I'm a step ahead of you." T-Mac held up a small earbud that would fit easily into her ear. "She could cover it with her hair."

Diesel took the earbud. "I believe we have a couple hours before the actual conference begins. I'd like to recon the area around the convention hall, find all the entrances and where they lead. If something goes down, we need to get Reese, Klein and as many of the attendees out of harm's way as quickly as possible."

"We can do that first and then find coffee," Big Jake said.

"You're hurting me, B.J.," Harm said.

T-Mac handed him a headset. "You'll live."

"Not unless I get a cup of coffee soon." Harm pressed the earpiece into his ear and slipped his arms into a button-down, short-sleeved cotton shirt. "Let's get this recon done soon. I have a date with a cuppa jo."

"I could do with a cup of coffee, too." Reese stepped out of the bedroom, wearing a sleek, gray jacket and slim-fitting, stretchy skirt that wouldn't hamper her movements.

All six men turned in her direction.

Diesel frowned at the hungry looks in their eyes. Hell, he couldn't blame them. She was beautiful.

She left her hair hanging down around her ears and shoulders, and she wore matching gray high-heeled shoes.

"Wow, you look like you could take on the United Nations in that getup," Buck said.

T-Mac whistled. "Dang, Diesel, I'd have gone for a run in the jungle if I'd known Reese was going with me, too."

Diesel's fists clenched. "Knock it off. She's here to do a job." He smiled. "Though, you do look like you could take on the entire conference and kick ass."

Reese blushed and smiled. "Thanks. All of you." She glanced at her watch. "I need to touch base with Ferrence. We'll probably go to breakfast in the hotel restaurant. I'd invite all of you to join us, but then everyone would know you're with us."

Buck sighed. "Have a couple of eggs over easy for me, will ya?"

"And a cup of black coffee for me," Harm said, giving up on the coffee maker the hotel provided each room.

Diesel handed Reese the earbud headset. "Try this on."

"What is it?"

"A two-way radio. You'll be able to contact us, and we can contact you."

She nodded and settled the communication device in her ear.

"Go ahead and try it," T-Mac said, pressing a similar earbud into his ear.

"Testing," Reese said. "Testing."

"I can hear you. Let's see if you can hear me." T-Mac stepped outside the hotel room and walked down the hallway.

Diesel closed the door.

Reese stared at Diesel, tipping her head to the side. "I can hear you," she said, smiling.

T-Mac opened the door. "You're good to go."

Reese tapped her ear. "Thanks." She glanced at Diesel's bare chest. "Are you coming with us?"

He nodded. "As far as I can."

"I doubt I can get you into the conference,

but you can join us for breakfast, since we've already established you as my fiancé."

"Fiancé?" Pitbull grinned. "Something you aren't telling us, dude?"

"Would you care to explain, while I finish dressing?" Diesel passed by Reese on his way to the bedroom.

Behind him, he heard Reese clear her throat. "Staying here was all part of his cover. Otherwise, he would have had to get a room somewhere farther away."

"Uh-huh," Buck said, a knowing grin spreading across his face. "Perfectly reasonable."

Diesel jammed his arms into the shirt, pulled on his socks and shoes and tucked in his shirt, in a hurry to get back to the sitting room before his teammates could further embarrass Reese. He buttoned his shirt and returned to the other room, handing his tie to Reese. "Could you?"

She wrapped the tie around his neck and made quick work of the knot at his throat. When she was done, she stood back. "Ready?"

He nodded and held out his arm. "I'll contact you guys later. Let me know what you find."

"Will do." Big Jake gave him a mock salute.

On his way out of the room, Diesel hung the Do Not Disturb sign on the outer doorknob.

Reese stepped across the hall and rapped on Klein's door.

Her client opened it, carrying a plain black briefcase and wearing a tailored charcoal-gray suit. "I was just about to come get you. I scored a breakfast with President Sabando's chief of staff. I hope to come out of breakfast having scheduled a meeting with the president himself." He handed the briefcase to Reese. "I'll need you to take notes."

"Do we need a translator?" she asked.

"No, he speaks English, having been educated at Harvard."

Diesel followed Reese and Klein to the hotel restaurant, where they met with Sabando's chief of staff, a tall, thin, dark man. He spoke English with an American accent.

A waiter led them to a table in the corner.

Diesel gave half of his attention to the conversation, while scanning the occupants of the restaurant.

So far, no one stood out as a threat. But then he didn't expect to find one yet. If anyone wanted to make the news, they'd wait until all the foreign dignitaries had arrived for the conference. Based on the number of Congolese soldiers at the social the night before, the conference center would be well guarded.

Still, Diesel felt better knowing part of his team would be there should anyone make a move on the delegates, Reese or Klein. He only wished they could have come armed. But then, how would they explain navy SEALs at a conference to which they weren't invited? The African Union might consider it a sign of aggression if they came in with their guns a-blazing. No, it was better they were unarmed and supposedly there on vacation. They didn't need to cause an international incident. And he knew his brothers—they'd have knives strapped to their ankles. They wouldn't be completely unarmed.

By the end of breakfast, Klein had his meeting scheduled for the day after the conference. He rose from the table, appearing quite pleased.

Sabando's chief of staff excused himself, claiming he needed to be available for the president when he arrived at the conference center.

Klein paid the bill. The three of them left and walked down the long hallway to the huge conference center attached to the hotel. Every twenty feet, they passed armed soldiers.

Other dignitaries and their entourages walked the long hall, as well. The conference would begin in less than thirty minutes. Dignitaries and their assistants hurried into the auditorium to take their assigned seats.

Reese and Klein checked in with the registration desk and were given badges to clip to their collars.

Diesel bent to kiss her and whispered. "I'll be waiting out here. But I'll be with you all the time."

She nodded and stood on her toes to kiss him again. Then she entered the auditorium behind Klein.

Diesel stood back far enough not to attract attention from the guards standing on either side of the entrance, weapons held at the ready.

Other members of dignitaries' entourages remained outside the auditorium, claiming seats on benches against the walls or pacing the corridors, talking quietly into their cell phones.

"Comm check," T-Mac said through Diesel's radio.

"Diesel here," he responded.

"Reese here," a whispered feminine voice said.

Diesel's heart swelled at the sound. "Damn, you sound sexy," he answered.

"Thank you. My momma always said I had a lady-killer voice," T-Mac responded.

"Jerk," Diesel said, a smile tugging at his lips.

He heard a feminine chuckle in his headset, warming him all over. Knowing they were in communication made him feel better about being separated from her, but he'd rather be seated next to her, in case someone got trigger-happy.

Other members of the team checked in, one by one.

"Pitbull here, sweetlips."

"Big Jake here," Big Jake reported. "Our check of the exterior of the conference center yielded three entrances—all heavily guarded by Congolese soldiers."

"Buck, here. Harm and I walked the connecting hallway earlier and counted three more entrances from inside. One of the doors leading off the far end of the hallway leads to a staircase down into the parking garage. As does an elevator. Parking garage has four levels below the convention center."

"They have guards at each of the levels checking people getting on and off the elevators or staircases."

The team had done well on their recon mission. Now all they could do was stand around and wait for something to happen that raised concern. They were men of action. Waiting would be a challenge. But, if Diesel had his way, they'd wait all day for nothing.

He'd rather have the day pass uneventfully than see problems arise with the conference attendees. Especially one named Reese Brantley.

Diesel paced the hallway, passing each of the three interior entrances. All three were guarded by two soldiers each. Minutes passed into one hour, and then two. Diesel didn't like being on the outside, away from Reese. What if someone had gotten past the guards? What if the fight started from within? None of the delegates were armed. They'd be cut down like fish in a bowl.

The longer he waited, the more worried he became, until he found himself standing in front of the door in which Reese and Klein had entered. The guards narrowed their eyes and tightened their grips on their weapons.

Chapter Ten

Reese sat beside Ferrence, silently watching the proceedings, listening in one ear to the interpreter through the headset she'd been given, while also straining to hear news on anything going on outside the conference center.

She'd studied the Congolese military men when she'd stepped through the doors of the auditorium. Two guards on the door didn't seem to be a lot. But then, she'd heard the team's report on those on the outside. Still, for the number of delegates at the meeting, she would have thought Sabando would have had more of a show of force in the streets.

"Harm here. I'm going farther out from the conference center to see if anything's happening in the streets. I'll circle around two or three blocks out."

"We'll cover the corners of the exterior," another one of the men reported.

On edge from the potential of hostilities, Reese was slightly comforted by the knowledge the SEALs were watching their backs. Though they were unarmed, they would provide a significant warning system should trouble arise outside the building.

"As the president of the Democratic Republic of the Congo, what are you doing about the human rights violations happening at the Metro mines?" The English interpreter translated the words of the female representative from Rwanda, who spoke directly to the DRC president in French.

Reese focused her attention on the president's response. He answered in French, the translation coming through moments later from the English interpreter.

President Sabando leaned into his microphone and answered with authority.

The interpreter translated, "I have my people looking into this."

"While your people are looking into it, men, women and children are dying. Young children under the age of ten are dying in those mines and have been for years. Why are you not doing anything to prevent this?" the woman asked.

Sabando lifted his chin, narrowing his eyes just a little before answering, "Policy moves slowly in this country. I am working on it. These people make their living working the mines. If we take away their living, they will starve."

The representative from Zambia spoke in English, "Food aid is available. Small children do not have to work in harsh conditions to eat."

"The rebels intercept the rations to these people. They are part of the problem," President Sabando replied.

The woman from Rwanda met Sabando's glare with a steady, unbending one of her own and spoke in rapid-fire French. The translator struggled to keep up, but the message was clear. "Rumor has it your military is intercepting the rations, not the rebels."

President Sabando pounded his fist on the table in front of him and fired back. The interpreter translated with the appropriate intonation. "Bosco Mutombo is responsible for stopping the food to the people. He steals from the people of the Democratic Republic of the Congo!"

"He claims he steals from your forces, taking the food away from them to give back to the people." The president's brother, Lawrence Sabando, entered the auditorium in full military regalia of the Congolese Army, speaking in English.

"He lies!" President Sabando stood so fast his chair fell over behind him. He pointed his finger at his brother and shouted in English. "And you would spread these lies because Mutombo works for you!"

"Tell the people of the African Union why you won't allow elections." The president's brother shook his fist. "Tell them!"

President Sabando stood tall, his chest puffed out, his chin held high. "Because the nation is unsettled. An election now would cause riots in the streets."

"There are already riots in the streets," his brother reasoned. "You can't control the change happening in our country. The people will prevail."

Riveted by the power struggle going on between the two brothers, Reese almost missed the change in stance of the guards surrounding the room. "We might have trouble inside the auditorium," she whispered, hoping the mic on her headset was sensitive enough to pick up her voice.

"Holy crap. Harm here. We have trouble coming in from the streets. A massive movement of people, who appear to be led by rebel forces, are on the march toward the conference center. Rebels are armed. Civilians have whatever they could get their hands on, from hunting rifles to axes and pitchforks. Must be a couple thousand."

Reese's heart leaped, and she stared around the room full of dignitaries, for a moment, at a loss for what to do.

"ETA?" Diesel's reassuring voice sounded in her ear.

"Two or three minutes before they arrive," he said, sounding as if he were running. "I'm closing ranks with the team."

"What should we do?" Reese asked.

"Get Klein to the south door," Diesel said. "The one to the far right of the door you entered."

"What about the rest of the delegates?" she asked.

Ferrence leaned close to her. "What's going on?"

Reese brought him up to date in a whisper. "We need to get out of here and seek shelter."

"If we stand up in the middle of the Sabandos' arguments, we'll draw too much attention."

"Did you hear that?" Reese asked into her mic.

"I don't care," Diesel said. "Get up and leave before things get hot on the inside, as well as the outside, of the auditorium."

"Going," Reese replied. Then she gripped Ferrence's hand tightly and shot him a stern stare. "Either you come with me now, or risk being trapped in this building when all hell breaks loose." She let go of him and gathered her notebook and pen, smiled at the people next to her and stood, hunkering low to keep from being too obvious.

She didn't get far before the shouting became more intense.

"You *will* hold elections on time, or the people will have their say," the president's brother yelled, fist waving in the air.

The president remained firm. "These people do not know what is good for them. They are uneducated. The country is not stable. Elections will cause chaos, I tell you."

"By not holding the elections as is mandated in our constitution, you will bring chaos down on all of us." Lawrence nodded toward one of the guards by the door.

The man raised his weapon and started firing over the heads of the crowd of delegates.

As soon as Reese saw the man raise his weapon, she grabbed Ferrence's arm and pushed him to the floor, covering his body with hers. "Get down," she yelled as loudly as she could. "Shots fired," she said, as if Diesel might not have heard the gunfire.

President Sabando dropped to the floor. "Are you insane?" he yelled to his brother.

"No, I'm determined to return the power to the people. This is a democratic republic, not a dictatorship. It is time for the tyrant to step down and be held accountable for his crimes!"

"This cannot be happening," Ferrence said, from his position beneath Reese. "I have an important meeting with the president tomorrow."

"Really?" Reese said, sliding to the side to poke her head up and assess the situation. "That's all you can think about when your life is in danger?" People were screaming and dropping to the floor.

"My father sent me here for one purpose.

If I'm not successful, for whatever reason, I'm a failure in his eyes."

"Cry me a river, Ferrence. I'm getting out of here alive, even if I have to take out a few of these gun-toting terrorists myself." She eyed the door Diesel had said to head for and mentally estimated forty feet between her and the door. "Look, Ferrence, we're getting out of here, either you come with me and stand a better chance of living, or stay here and die."

"Either way, I doubt I'll get that meeting with Sabando. I wonder, if his brother takes over, can I meet with him instead?"

"For the love of Mike!" Reese cursed.

Ferrence struggled to his feet, bent over and followed Reese as she crossed the room toward the south door.

More shots were fired, echoing off the walls. Delegates cried out and rushed for the doors, pushing Reese and Ferrence in front of them.

Two men with guns blocked their path, pointing their weapons toward them.

Reese pretended to trip, falling into one of the men, shoving his weapon toward the ceiling. She performed her best side kick, aiming for the other man's hands. His weapon jettisoned out of his hands and clattered to the floor. Meanwhile, Reese fought for control of the guy pointing his weapon toward the ceiling. He elbowed her in the side of the head, knocking her earbud out. Knowing she was running out of time and the other men with weapons would start firing at her across the room, she shoved her thumbs in the man's eyes and lifted her knee with a swift upward jerk, kneeing him in the groin. The man went down, his grip loosening on the rifle. Reese wrested it from his grip and flung it away.

His partner lunged for Reese, but one of the delegates blocked him by swinging his briefcase up, hitting him in the nose. Blood spurted, and the gunman's eyes watered. He went down, clutching his face in his hands.

With nothing standing between them and the door, Reese grabbed one of the rifles from the ground and rushed forward. She shoved through the door and ran out. While the rebels focused on the delegates and the president still back in the auditorium, Reese ran for the door on the opposite side of the wall. From what the SEAL team said, it would lead to the parking garage below. Reese held the door for Ferrence. "Go down as far as you can and hide. I'm right behind you."

Before she could follow him, delegates shoved her out of the way, ran through the door and hurried down the stairs. Then the president of the Democratic Republic of the Congo appeared in front of her. "Who are you?" he demanded in English.

"Does it matter? If you want to be safe, follow me," Reese commanded.

The president nodded and hurried down the steps after her. Reese glanced over her shoulder. The last one through the door above was the president's brother, Lawrence Sabando.

She knew it would mean more trouble, but she had to get these people and Ferrence to safety. She'd deal with the troublemakers later. Then the door to the auditorium slammed shut, and no more delegates emerged. Several men dressed in shabby rebel camouflage uniforms rushed toward them.

Reese ran down the stairs, following the slower moving delegates. At the rate they were moving, the terrorists would catch up and shoot her first. And since the president was with her, she might as well have a bright red target painted on her back.

All she'd been paid to do was keep track of

Ferrence Klein, be his assistant and protect him. Had she known she'd be at the center of a national coup attempt, she might have told the Kleins where they could go with their money. But second-guessing herself wouldn't get her out of the current situation. She had to use her brain and her fighting skills to see herself through and get Ferrence safely back to the States.

She didn't have time to think about Diesel and his teammates, unarmed and at the mercy of the terrorists. But she couldn't help wondering if they got out all right, or if they were in the midst of the fighting.

A loud crashing sound echoed down the stairwell. Voices shouted above, and someone fired shots that pinged off the concrete steps.

"Go! Go! Go!" Reese shouted to the people in front of her.

The people up front had reached the bottom of the staircase and spilled out into the lowest level of the parking garage. It wouldn't take long for the gunmen to get to them. They had to find a place to hide.

"Ferrence!" she yelled, anxious to get to him. Her job was to protect him, and she couldn't do it with all the others in the way.

"Over here!" Ferrence shouted. He held open

a door marked with red lettering in French and English—Authorized Personnel Only.

With nowhere else to go but being out in the open in a free-for-all coup, Reese had no choice. "Get inside! Go!" She waved at the delegates and the president as if they were children who were slow to come off the playground. No one seemed to understand the urgency but Reese and Ferrence.

The squeal of car tires screamed off the concrete walls of the parking garage, heading lower in the building. They only had seconds to get everyone through the door and find some way of locking it behind them.

WHEN DIESEL HEARD Harm's assessment of the outside situation, he'd immediately told Reese to get out. He walked up to the doors and was barred from entering by the two guards dressed in DRC uniforms. He saw no other way to get past them but to start a fight. As he balled his fists, ready to throw the first punch, gunshots rang out inside the auditorium.

The guards turned toward the doors, weapons at the ready.

"What's going on in there?" Big Jake asked.

"Shots fired inside the auditorium. I'm

going in." Diesel shoved the guards from behind, pushing them into the melee of the auditorium.

More shots were fired from similarly dressed guards on the inside. The president of the DRC was running low to the ground, shouting orders like a football quarterback, while the delegates either lay flat on the ground or ran screaming for the doors.

Through the chaos, Diesel had a hard time locating Reese. Then, he spotted her on the far end of the large auditorium, taking out the two guards blocking her exit. She'd done as he'd told her and made for the south exit. *Good girl!*

Diesel would have cheered out loud at her skill and bravery, but bullets flew, and he had to get down or get shot. As soon as he was certain Reese and Klein made it out, Diesel backed toward the doorway he'd entered.

"The north end of the building has been breached," Big Jake said into Diesel's radio headset. "I repeat, the building has been breached."

"We need weapons," Buck lamented. "Without them, we're useless."

"Do your best to get the delegates to safety,"

Diesel said. "There are only a few gunmen in the auditorium."

"There are a lot more people with guns rushing the north entrance," Harm said.

"Get into the auditorium and block the entrances," Diesel said, heading for the north door where he took out the gunman, and used his rifle to jam the doors shut.

"That might mean taking out some of the DRC military guys," Buck said.

"Do what it takes, otherwise this event will turn into a serious international incident," Big Jake said.

"Roger," Buck replied. Harm, T-Mac and Pitbull chimed in.

A moment later the outside doors burst open, and the team stormed in. They only took a few moments to disarm the guards inside, and then they locked the doors from the inside.

Within seconds, voices shouted from outside, and people banged on the metal doors.

"We have to get the delegates out of here, before they try blowing the doors open," Diesel said. "I'm going for the south exit. Pitbull, T-Mac, come with me. The rest of you, herd the dignitaries to the south exit."

"Where's Reese?" Buck asked.

"She made it out, and I'm guessing she headed down the stairs to the parking garage. I haven't heard from her. She might have lost her comm."

"There were rioters pouring into the garage on the north side," Harm said. "They were swarming the streets like ants. Without weapons, we'll be lucky to make it out of this alive."

"Don't be a Debby Downer, Harm," Big Jake said. "We'll make it, and these delegates will, too."

"Not this one," Buck hovered over a man lying on his back, staring up at the ceiling. "No blood. Looks like he suffered a massive heart attack."

"Do what you can for those who've been injured," Diesel said, "but get those who can move up and out of here as soon as we clear a path."

"Where's President Sabando?" Big Jake asked.

Diesel's heart sank. "He must have made it out with Reese and Klein." Which meant he'd draw the fight to him and Reese. The rebels might not be discriminating when shooting at the president. Reese could become collateral damage.

Diesel crossed to the south exit, took a deep breath, unlocked the door and peered out. Several terrorists dressed in ragged camouflage uniforms were crowding into the stairwell leading into the garage.

One of them spotted Diesel and swung his rifle around too late.

Diesel rushed across the hallway, pushed the rifle up toward the ceiling and punched the man in the throat. He fell, clutching at his shattered windpipe, gasping for air. The man behind him spun and fired off several rounds without first aiming. The bullets hit the wall. Diesel hit the shooter, knocking him backward and down the stairs, taking out two more men already on their way down. That sent them tumbling to a heap at the landing, their weapons flying to the side.

Before they could scramble to their feet, Diesel, T-Mac and Pitbull had their rifles and were pointing them in their faces.

Diesel left the others and continued down the steps. T-Mac and Pitbull would spend a few precious moments tying their wrists and feet with the zip ties T-Mac always kept handy.

Diesel hurried downward, listening as he went. He could hear the squeal of tires and the sounds of footsteps pounding on the concrete floors at the upper levels, but he couldn't hear the sounds of voices from the fleeing delegates or Reese.

He worried he'd come the wrong way, except the rebel fighters had been on their way down, as well. They had to be after someone. From the sound of footsteps on the stairs below, there might be some of the rebels getting too close for comfort to the woman he'd made love to the night before. He couldn't let anything happen to her. Now that he'd found the feisty, former MMA fighter, he didn't want to let her go. She was everything he could ever want in a woman—independent, strong and determined. Only a confident woman like her, familiar with the military life, stood a chance of making a relationship with a SEAL last. Perhaps he could find a way to make something between them work—if only he were given the chance.

Chapter Eleven

Reese rammed the pointy heel of her shoe into the doorjamb and closed the door hard, hoping to slow her pursuers. When she turned to survey the room she found herself in, she frowned. Pipes hung from the ceiling, and machines filled the room. These were the heating, air, water supply and other mechanical devices necessary to operate a huge hotel and convention center.

In the middle of the room, Lawrence Sabando faced off with his brother, Jean-Paul, the president of the DRC.

"If the rebellion is successful," the president said, as he poked a finger at his brother's chest, "you will be responsible for this country's disastrous fall into chaos."

"Better than being ruled by a tyrant," Lawrence responded. "Your time is finished as president."

"The country isn't stable," Jean-Paul argued. "Having an election will cause great unrest."

"We are brothers, but we must do what we must." Lawrence held out his hand, as if to shake his brother's.

The president's eyes narrowed, but he took his brother's hand.

Lawrence gripped his brother's hand and shook it. "A man must do what a man must do." Before Jean-Paul could pull his hand free, his brother twisted his free arm up behind his back and pulled a pistol from beneath his jacket.

Reese was too far away from the two men to interfere with what was happening.

Jean-Paul cried out, "What is this?"

"I'm taking the country back for the people."

"You do not know what you are doing." The president stood on his toes to relieve the pressure on his arm. "My army will slaughter your rebels."

"Not if you tell them to back down," his brother replied.

"I will not."

"Then you will die, and our people will elect a new leader."

Reese couldn't believe what was happening. As if they didn't have enough problems outside the door to the room they hid in. Inside could get just as messy. Reese had to do something before the situation spiraled out of her control. "Uh, sirs."

Ferrence stepped forward, closer to the two men than Reese. "Maybe we can talk this out peacefully."

Lawrence swung his gun toward Ferrence. "All you want is to get your hands on our minerals. You don't care about our country."

"I care about getting out of this alive," Ferrence said. "As I'm sure your brother does."

Reese glanced around the room at the frightened dignitaries. "Look, there are a lot of people in here," she said. "Could you take your argument where others won't be hurt?"

Lawrence snorted. "Foolish woman. Other countries have hovered like vultures, preying on our natural resources, raping the lands of what is ours. The people of the Democratic Republic of the Congo deserve to be free of oppression from my brother, from the countries that would force our people into slavery, and make our children work in the mines from the day they learn to walk to the day they die. This ends now."

A shot rang out.

Reese dropped to the ground. Only, the sound came from behind them. Pounding sounded on the door, and then the door burst open, her shoe having done little to keep the rebels out.

Three men rushed in, pointing rifles at the dignitaries huddled in a corner.

Lawrence said something in Lingala and then waved his gun toward the hostages. "You will follow these men out of this room and into the van waiting in the parking garage."

Reese glanced around the room, looking for anything she could use as a weapon.

Lawrence's eyes narrowed. "If you do not do exactly as I say, my men are instructed to kill one delegate at a time to gain your compliance." His gaze settled on Ferrence and then Reese. "Who will be first?"

Reese held up her hands. "I'll do whatever you say. Just don't shoot these people."

"I'm not arguing," Ferrence said. "You want me to go into a van? I'll go." He started for the door and stopped when a man blocked his path.

Reese gasped when she realized it was Diesel, standing on the other side of the threshold. "Don't try anything," she called out. "They have their weapons trained on the delegates."

Diesel ducked back out of the doorframe.

Seconds later, a shot was fired, whizzed past Reese's ear and splintered the doorframe, inches from where Diesel had been standing a moment before, but was now gone.

Reese gasped and held her breath, praying the bullet hadn't ricocheted off the door and hit Diesel.

"Stay close together," Lawrence said.

His men shoved their rifles into the backs of some of the dignitaries, herding them out of the room and into the garage.

A dark van skidded around a corner and came to a stop, steps away from the door.

When Reese stepped out of the room, she shot a glance around, searching for Diesel. He was nowhere to be seen.

"Don't try anything, or we will shoot the delegates," Lawrence called out in English, and then in French.

More rebel fighters filled the garage, surrounding them. Outside on the street, sounds of gunfire made it feel like an all-out war was going on.

"You will not get away with this," the president said. "My men will kill you and your rebels."

Lawrence shook his head. "Not if I have you as a hostage." He pressed the handgun to his brother's head. "Get in the van," he called out to the delegates.

One by one, they climbed into the van, until it was packed with people. Then four armed men climbed in with them.

When Reese and Ferrence started to get in, Lawrence stopped them.

"No. You two will come with me and my brother." Lawrence nodded toward a group of men. "Follow me."

A mob of armed men gathered around Lawrence, his brother, Reese and Ferrence. Together, they reentered the conference building. In their strange little huddle, they walked down the long hallway, passing other members of their rebellion, until they reached the elevator bay.

Lawrence touched the button with the barrel of his pistol.

When the door opened, Lawrence shoved his brother in first, holding tightly to his arm, with his gun pressed to his head. He turned and nodded toward Reese and Ferrence. "Get in, or I kill my brother, and then I'll kill one of you."

Ferrence and Reese entered simultaneously, and five of the rebels crowded in behind them, all carrying wicked-looking guns. The doors closed.

"Take us to the top, brother," Lawrence said. "I know you only reserve the best with the people's money."

"I don't have my key," Jean-Paul said.

"Then I suppose you will die." Lawrence pressed the gun harder to his brother's head and started to squeeze the trigger.

"Okay, okay, it's in my pocket. Don't shoot!" the president cried. With his free hand, he pulled his key card out of his pocket, waved it in front of the control panel and hit the button for the top floor.

As the elevator rose through the building, Reese wondered when and where this would end and whether Diesel had been hit. If this was the end for her, she wished she could see him one last time.

Reese wouldn't let this be the end for her or her client. She'd been to hell and back and survived. She'd be damned if it was all for naught. She had to think she was in this position, at this time, for a reason. And that reason was to get her client out of hot water and get herself back home.

When they emerged from the elevator, Lawrence urged them to climb the stairs to the rooftop, where a helicopter touched down in front of them.

Lawrence waved Reese and Ferrence toward the helicopter. Once they were inside, he shoved his brother into a seat. Two other guards climbed in and pointed their rifle barrels at Reese and Ferrence.

As the helicopter lifted off the roof, Reese sat back in her helicopter seat, buckled her safety harness and went through every scenario that would get her and Ferrence out of this mess. She would not go down without a fight. First, they needed to be on the ground again, where they had a chance of escaping. Then she'd have to convince Ferrence to go along with her plan. Whatever that plan might be. She couldn't wait for the SEAL team to find her. They might not make it in time.

"T-Mac, TELL ME you still have GPS tracking on Klein and Reese." Diesel, T-Mac and Pitbull managed to get the hell out of the parking garage before the rebel forces converged on them.

"I've got Klein. Last night, while you were picking your noses, I snuck into Klein's room and planted a tracker in his watch," T-Mac confirmed.

"You have the GPS tracking device?"

"In my duffel bag back, in the hotel room." T-Mac stopped and stared at the hotel surrounded by the mob of rebels and civilians. "How the hell are we going to get inside?"

"Service entrance." They worked their way around the crowd of rebels converging on the hotel to the back, where trucks were backed up to loading docks, their drivers having deserted the area. The team entered through an open overhead door and slipped down a service hallway.

Ahead, they saw a crowd of people heading their way.

"In here." Diesel ducked into a huge laundry room. T-Mac and Pitbull darted through the door and turned to see who was coming.

"I'll be damned," Pitbull said and opened the door right as the first person in line passed the door. He reached out and grabbed a man, dragging him into the laundry room. The man came in fighting.

Pitbull ducked a punch. "Buck, it's me," he said.

Buck stopped with his arm half-cocked, ready to throw another punch. "Pitbull?" He glanced around. "Damn, where did you guys come from?"

"Long story," Diesel peeked out into the hallway, where more delegates stood, worried frowns on their faces. At least these hadn't been bundled into a van and carted off to who knew where. "Where's Big Jake and Harm?"

"That you, Diesel?" At the back of the group, Big Jake looked over the tops of the delegates' heads.

"Bring them in here," Diesel said.

Big Jake and Harm herded the dignitaries into the laundry room.

"I think they'll be all right in here until the riot dissipates," Diesel said. "We have to find Klein and Reese."

"I thought you had them covered," Buck said.

"Until Lawrence hijacked them. He loaded a van full of delegates going to who knows where."

T-Mac held up a hand. "I slapped a magnetic GPS tracker on that van as it was driving out of the parking garage."

Diesel grinned. "Damn, you're good. But that doesn't account for Reese and Klein. We need to get the tracking device."

"We passed the utility elevator on our way through. Come on." Buck checked the hallway and waved to the others.

The team ran for the elevator, while Big Jake stayed back to warn the dignitaries to stay put until the rioting was over. By the time the elevator had arrived and the five men had stepped in, Big Jake came around the corner and hopped on board. The elevator rose to their floor at what felt like the pace of ice freezing. By the time the doors opened, Diesel had ground the enamel off his back teeth.

Reese could be anywhere in the DRC. The longer it took to find her, the farther away she could be.

Inside the suite, Diesel raced T-Mac to the duffel bag and waited for his teammate to dig out the tracking device and turn it on.

He frowned down at the screen. "It appears as though Klein is right on top of us."

"What do you mean?"

"The tracker is two-dimensional. They could be at the bottom of the building, the top or on any one of the floors." His frown deepened.

"What?" Diesel demanded.

"They're moving."

"As in, driving out onto the street?" Buck asked.

"No. As if cutting across the city, going fast." T-Mac turned toward the window. "There!" He pointed to the sky.

A helicopter flew past the window and away toward the east.

"Damn!" Diesel pulled his cell phone from his suit jacket.

"If you're hoping to get more help, they won't send any more assistance from Djibouti," Big Jake said.

"I'm not calling Djibouti." He scrolled through his contacts and found the one he was looking for. "I'm calling Marly."

"Bush flights, Marly speaking," a voice answered on the second ring.

"Marly, it's Diesel. Please tell me you're still at the airport."

"I am. I just finished filing my flight plan back to Zambia."

"File another to somewhere east."

"I have to be a little more specific."

"Pick a city. I don't care. Reese and Klein have been taken by Sabando's brother in a helicopter headed east. I need you to follow them."

"They could be going anywhere. By the time you get to the airport, they will be long gone."

"We have a tracker on Klein."

"Well, why didn't you say so?" Marly said. "Get your ass to the airport ASAP. I'll have the plane ready to go."

"Will it hold six men plus you?"

"Easily. Why?" she asked. "Did you make some friends in Kinshasa?"

Diesel glanced around at his teammates, glad they were in this together. "You could say that."

"Bring them. I'll be waiting." Marly ended the call.

While T-Mac gathered their equipment into his duffel bag, Diesel shed his suit, slipped on jeans, a T-shirt and the boots he'd purchased when he'd been out the day before. In less than two minutes, he was heading for the door, backpack in hand, carrying his dismantled M4A1 rifle. "Let's go. We have a damsel in distress to rescue."

"Oh, so now we're in the knights-in-shining-armor business?" Pitbull asked. "Do we get to bring out our weapons for this one?"

"You bet." Diesel ran for the utility elevator and punched the down button. Fortunately, the elevator doors opened immediately, and the men piled in.

On the ride down, Diesel clenched and unclenched his fists, his insides knotted so tightly, he could barely breathe. Why had Lawrence separated Reese and Klein from the dignitaries? And why did he feel the need to take them with him to wherever he planned on disposing of his brother?

"How are we getting from the hotel to the airport?" T-Mac asked.

"We'll get clear of the riot and see if we can grab a taxi," Big Jake answered.

Diesel was thankful his team was there with him. They helped to keep him together when he felt like coming apart at the seams. Normally level-headed when going into a dangerous situation, he was completely out of his element now. All because of a woman who'd slipped beneath his defenses and stolen a part of him.

Holy hell.

Diesel shook his head. Could it be? Had she stolen his heart in the few short days they'd known each other? Falling in love could not have happened so fast. Before Reese, he wasn't sure he even believed love existed. Lust? Well, yeah. But love?

He felt as if someone had sucker punched him in the gut. Was that what love felt like? Why would anyone want to feel like that?

Reese had been taken away in a helicopter to God knew where. If they didn't find her quickly, it might be too late.

The doors opened, and Diesel rushed out. He led the way to the loading docks and down backstreets not already crowded with rioters or rebels. He could hear the reassuring sound of footsteps pounding behind him, and he felt glad his team had his back.

Four blocks from the hotel and conference center, they were able to hail two taxis. The drivers promised to hurry toward the airport.

Hurry was relative. In the congested streets, nothing moved fast.

By the time the taxis dropped them at the airport, Diesel was so wound up, he leaped out of the cab and ran for the flight line where Marly's plane sat waiting for them.

Marly stood outside of the aircraft, talking to several DRC soldiers wielding rifles.

Diesel slowed to a more casual walk and waved at Marly. "What's going on?"

"These men want to take my plane, but I explained to them we're about to take off on an emergency flight to save a life."

"You are the doctor?" one of the soldiers asked.

Diesel met Marly's gaze, and then the soldier's. "Yes, sir."

"And these men?" The soldier glanced over Diesel's shoulder.

"All in the medical field." Big Jake stepped up beside Diesel. "An entire village has come down with the Ebola virus. We're on our way in to help." The man towered everyone standing on the tarmac. "Would you care to accompany us?"

The leader of the DRC soldiers tipped his head up and squinted at Big Jake for a long moment. Then he shook his head. "No, we will find another airplane. Carry on."

Marly waved to the plane. "You can store your bags in the wing compartment. The sooner we board, the sooner I can get clearance from the tower."

T-Mac loaded his duffel bag into the wing,

and the men climbed aboard the aircraft. Diesel sat in the copilot's seat beside Marly, settled the headset over his ears and held the GPS tracking device like a lifeline to Reese.

Marly started the engine, contacted the air traffic controller and waited for clearance to take off.

Moments later, they were airborne.

"Which way?" she asked.

"East."

She rolled her eyes. "I don't suppose you can be more specific?"

"Not really. Right now, it appears they are flying due east and they have a sizable head start on us."

Marly nodded. "That works for now. I filed flight plans to Kananga, which is due east. Let me know if their direction changes."

They passed over farmland, jungle and rivers. Every so often, Diesel would inform Marly of slight changes to their route.

She adjusted and pushed on.

By nightfall, their fuel was getting low, and the helicopter ahead of them was slowing. They were about thirty minutes behind the craft carrying Reese and Ferrence.

"I need to land at an airport, where I can refuel," Marly said. "There's one in Kamenbe."

Diesel checked the tracker. "They stopped."

Marly glanced at the device. "Even if I could land there, I wouldn't have enough fuel to take off again and get to the nearest airport with facilities to refuel. I'll have to overshoot their landing area and go on to Kamenbe."

Diesel nodded, his fingers clenched so tightly around the tracker, his knuckles turned white. Marly was right. They couldn't land where the helicopter did, even if they had enough fuel. "T-Mac, you don't happen to have a parachute hidden away in that duffel bag of yours, do you?"

"Wouldn't matter if I did—it's stored in the wing."

"Damn. I hate being so close, but so far," he said. "Can we at least fly over the landing site so that we can see what we're shooting for?"

Marly nodded. "You bet. But if you don't mind, I'd rather not get in range of small arms fire." She reached into a compartment and extracted a pair of binoculars. "Here."

Diesel pressed the binoculars to his eyes. As they neared the location where the green blip was on the tracking device, Diesel glanced out the window.

The terrain had changed from jungle to huge scars on the land, where open-pit mining craters had been dug.

He could see the helicopter below. A couple of SUVs were pulling away from the aircraft.

The helicopter rose slowly from the ground, rising into the air.

"That's our cue to get the heck out of here. That chopper has guns on it." Marly increased the plane's speed, sending it on its way to Kamenbe.

All the while, Diesel studied the land, the roads leading into and out of villages along the way. He noted several trucks full of men in military uniforms, carrying rifles and what appeared to be rocket-propelled grenades. The trucks stirred up dust along the roads, heading toward the mine. Diesel wondered if they were part of Jean-Paul's army or the rebels fighting with Lawrence? Either way, they could stir up more trouble for Reese and Klein.

Since the helicopter was taking off, and the green blip wasn't moving with it, Diesel thought it could be safe to bet Ferrence and Reese were still on the ground. Their best plan would be to get to Kamenbe, rent, borrow or steal a vehicle and get back out to the mine, and soon, before they could move the captives again.

Chapter Twelve

Reese wished she had on a sturdy pair of trousers and her hiking boots. Dressed in a skirt suit, barefooted because she'd ditched her heels in order to run and jam a door, she wasn't in any condition to make good an escape.

What she didn't understand was why Lawrence had brought them all the way across the country to what appeared to be an open-pit mine. If he were going to kill them, wouldn't he have done it already?

She didn't want to get her hopes up, but Lawrence might not be as bad as she originally thought. Perhaps he only wanted to teach his brother and the greedy Americans a lesson. Reese hoped that was the extent of his plan and that he would then turn them loose.

In the meantime, she wasn't counting on it. She had to have a plan B.

The helicopter was met by two Land Rovers. Lawrence, his brother and two soldiers climbed into the first with the driver. Rebel soldiers nudged Reese and Ferrence with the barrels of their weapons, herding them toward the other SUV. Now would be a good time to fight her way free, but she didn't have shoes, and the rebel fighters didn't appear to have a sense of humor. They'd probably shoot rather than ask permission. Reese and Ferrence climbed into the back seat with one of the fighters. Another fighter sat in the front, turned around in his seat with a pistol and pointed it at Ferrence's chest.

"I hope we don't hit any major bumps along the way," Ferrence whispered.

"Quiet!" The soldier beside Ferrence hit him in the jaw with his elbow.

Ferrence pressed a hand to his jaw and closed his mouth. They drove several miles, deeper and deeper into the maze of open-pit mines. The sun had long since descended from its zenith, now casting long shadows, as it raced for the horizon.

The vehicle in front of them finally halted in front of what might once have been a white tent. The white canvas was stained a muddy red from the dust kicked up by vehicles and mining activities.

Rebel fighters crowded around the tent, shouting something in Lingala. Lawrence ushered his brother, whose hands had been bound behind his back.

A cheer went up from the fighters, and shots were fired into the air.

Reese cringed. All it took was one careless fighter to swing a weapon their direction, pull the trigger and boom. Reese held her breath as she was escorted into the tent. Once inside, a rebel fighter bound her wrists in front of her with a strap and bound Ferrence's behind his back and forced him to kneel so that they could bind his ankles. *Apparently, a woman in a skirt suit wasn't as scary as a man.* Reese counted her blessings. She was one step closer to escape. She could easily untie Ferrence's restraints, and he could return the favor, as soon as their captors left them alone for any length of time.

"I don't understand why you have brought me here. If you're going to kill me, why not get it over with?" The president had been bound much like Ferrence, his wrists behind his back. He sat on the ground, with his knees drawn up and his ankles tied together.

"I want you to see what you have done to this country by your actions or, rather, inaction. You have sold this country to the devils." Lawrence glared at Ferrence and Reese. "The Americans will know, too, what price our people have paid. When the sun rises again, you will see."

Lawrence left the tent and gave brief orders to his men in Lingala.

From the shadows on the outside of the tent, Reese could tell there were two rebel fighters left as guards, one on either end. The two guards inside the tent sat on boxes, facing them, their rifles resting on their laps.

As the sun sank below the horizon, the interior of the tent went from gray to black. The inside guards stood, stretched, said something in their language and headed for the tent's flap door.

Outside, they spoke to the guards on the front and then left.

As soon as the inside guards left the tent, Reese tore at the bindings on her wrists with her teeth, working the knots in an attempt to loosen them. She stopped when one of the two guards standing outside ducked his head into the tent and shined a flashlight at the captives.

Reese raised her hands to block the glare.

The guard stared at her suit and snorted. He then left the tent and said something to the other guard, and they laughed.

Reese hoped her skirt suit gave them some form of entertainment that would keep them occupied long enough for her to tear the knots loose. There were several SUVs outside the tent. If she could get to one of those, she and Ferrence might have a way out—if she didn't get lost in the maze of roads through the mining operations.

Reese struggled with the strap, but no matter how hard she tried to pull with her teeth, the strap wasn't coming loose. She'd looked around the tent, while there was still light left from the sun, but hadn't found anything that appeared to be sharp enough to cut through the leather. If she could get to the wooden crates the guards had used as seats, she might be able to rub the straps against the coarse edges of the wooden slats.

Someone outside the tent lit a fire, giving just enough light for Reese to find her way. Not sure if the campfire would silhouette her movements against the tent, she crossed the dirt floor on her knees, a little at a time, until she was next to a crate. Thankfully, the boards it was made of were rough-hewn and provided a serrated edge to rub her bonds against.

"What are you doing?" Ferrence whispered.

"Trying to get us out of here," she answered.

"And how far will we get?" Ferrence asked. "You're barefooted, and we're surrounded by men with guns."

"They will shoot you if you step one foot outside of this tent," Jean-Paul said, his lip pulled back in a sneer. "You should wait for my army to come to our rescue. They will be here soon."

The president had confidence his troops would find him and carry him back to Kinshasa and safety.

Reese, not so much. The riots in the streets of the capital city were evidence the country was already in turmoil. The president had not helped matters by delaying the elections. He'd angered his people and possibly some of the members of the country's armed forces. They might let this be a lesson to anyone who tried again to circumvent the constitutional elections.

"We can wait for morning and whatever Lawrence wants us to see, and then be shot, or get out in the dark of night and maybe live to tell our grandchildren about our adventure." Reese pushed harder against the crate. The leather strap seemed to be thicker and stronger than she'd originally thought. At the rate she was going, it would be morning before she broke through.

Ferrence scooted across to where she sat and turned his back to her. "See if you can untie mine."

She stopped long enough to work at the strap they'd used to tie Ferrence's wrists together. His was some kind of synthetic material, but equally strong. The knot was so tight, no amount of coaxing with her fingers so close together would work it loose.

"You'll have to rub yours on the crate, too." Reese went back to scraping her strap against the wood.

Ferrence turned his back to the second wooden crate and started rubbing his bindings against the wood. He faced Reese as they worked. "Do you think your fiancé will be able to find us?"

Her heart fluttered at Ferrence's reference to her fiancé. Diesel wasn't her fiancé, but the sound of the word on her client's lips almost made it seem real and exciting. *Foolish*, she realized. "I don't know. We've come a long way. They'd have had to find someone to fly them here."

"I saw how you handled the guards in the conference center. And you got us out of the last situation like a pro." Ferrence stared at her in the limited lighting, his eyes narrowed. "You're not just an assistant, are you?"

"You father hired me to be your assistant on this trip. That's what I am," Reese hedged. Why did it matter now that she'd been hired as a bodyguard? Once again, she felt she'd failed her client. She hoped she would be as fortunate this time as she was the last time, and that they were able to get out of hot water and back to safety. If they ever got back to the States, she'd really have to rethink her career choice and come up with a better plan.

Time passed, and she still hadn't managed to tear through her restraints. Hunger gnawed at her belly, and exhaustion wore her down. Still, she rubbed until her wrists were raw and her eyelids closed of their own accord. Her last thought was of Diesel. She prayed he'd gotten out of the city alive and that his team made it out, as well. She also prayed she'd see him again. She'd tell him how much their short time together had meant to her, even if it hadn't meant as much to him.

MARLY LANDED THE little plane at the Ka- menbe Airport, just after dusk.

Big Jake was able to rent a large enough black SUV to get all of them inside. Diesel took the wheel, too wound up, and in need of something to keep his mind off what could be happening to Reese, to sit in the back seat, gnawing at his fingernails.

The roads back to the mines started out paved, but quickly became gravel, and then dirt. Dust sifted through every opening of the SUV, even though they traveled with the windows up.

Big Jake rode shotgun and T-Mac sat in the middle, holding the GPS tracker in his lap, while studying the one provided at the rental car agency. They'd paid for the insurance, un- sure as to what shape the vehicle would be in when they returned it— *if* they returned it.

"We should have called back to Djibouti for air transport," T-Mac said.

"We never were supposed to be in the DRC," Big Jake said. "Transporting the SOC-R onto the Congo River was a huge risk. Bringing helicopters to the big cities would draw even more attention, and it could end up on the nightly news."

Diesel didn't say anything. He was with T-Mac, wishing they had a faster, more direct way to get to Reese. Instead, they were stuck on dirt roads, traveling through the night, hoping they were going the right way. As the roads narrowed, they had to do some backtracking, which wasted even more time.

In the early hours of the morning, T-Mac nodded off, his head dipping so sharply, it woke him immediately. He yawned, stretched and glanced down at the tracking device. "We should be getting pretty close."

"Close, as in a mile or two, or close, as in within the same continent?" Diesel asked, getting crankier by the minute. Time was passing all too quickly, and they still hadn't made it to the mining operation. Everything appeared so different in the dark. He might drive off the edge of an open-pit mine for all he knew.

"As in, within five miles. We might consider hiding the SUV and going the rest of the way on foot soon. We don't want the rebel fighters to open fire on the strange vehicle entering their space in the dead of night."

"Let's get another mile closer, and then we'll ditch the vehicle," Diesel said.

"Turn out the headlights, then, so they don't see us coming," Big Jake suggested.

Diesel slowed almost to a stop before extinguishing the headlights. He took a few minutes to allow his eyesight to adjust to the darkness.

"Guys, wake up back there." T-Mac twisted in his seat. "Get the night vision goggles out of the duffel bag. We might need them sooner than you think."

Diesel glanced in the rearview mirror at his teammates.

Pitbull, Buck and Harm sat up instantly.

Harm reached behind the seat and pulled the duffel bag over into his lap with a grunt. "Damn, T-Mac what *don't* you have in this bag of tricks?" He passed forward a pair of night vision goggles.

T-Mac handed them to Big Jake.

Jake slipped the night vision goggles over his eyes and scanned the road ahead.

Now that his sight had adjusted to nothing but the limited light from the stars overhead, he picked up speed, eating up the next two miles.

"They're close," T-Mac said.

Diesel found a good spot on the side of the road where he could hide the SUV. They'd go in on foot from here. Finally, he'd be able to help Reese.

Once they covered the SUV in brush and branches, the team took off through the trees and bushes, paralleling the road, still following the GPS tracker. When they were within half a mile of the bright green dot on the tracking device, they slowed and took even more care to locate any outlying sentries.

Harm, Pitbull and Big Jake manned the night vision goggles and spread out, searching for anyone lying in wait of people entering the perimeter of the mining camp.

"Got a heat signature near the road, fifty meters ahead," Pitbull reported.

"Another on the opposite side of the road. Appears to be lying down. Could be asleep," Big Jake said. "Going in."

"Same here," Pitbull acknowledged.

"On three," Big Jake whispered into the radio. "One...two...three."

Without night vision goggles to see the green heat signature of bodies moving ahead, Diesel had to rely on his own eyesight. All he could see was a couple of gray shadows moving in the woods, and only because he knew what he was looking for.

"Target subdued," Big Jake reported.

"Make that two," Pitbull seconded. "All clear up to the camp. Bound forward. We have your six."

With Big Jake and Pitbull covering, Diesel, Harm, Buck and T-Mac bounded forward, almost to the very edge of the camp.

The camp was a mass of tents and shacks made of discarded plywood, pieces of corrugated tin and other trash.

At the far end was a large white tent, tinged blue by the moonlight.

"Based on the tracker, Klein is in or very near that tent," T-Mac said.

"And, if they kept them together, Reese should be with him," Diesel said, thinking optimistically. Though they really had no reason to keep her alive. She wasn't the bargaining chip. She didn't have a father with a vast fortune to negotiate her release. Still, Diesel wouldn't give up hope. Reese had to be with Klein. And he'd bet his last dollar she had an escape plan.

"Our biggest problem now is getting past all the people between us and the white tent," Big Jake said.

Diesel stared at the dark camp. "What do you mean?"

Big Jake moved up beside Diesel and handed him the night vision goggles.

Diesel stared through the lenses. "Damn."

In amongst the tents, plywood shacks and garbage were people—whether lying beneath a shelter, out in the open, or sleeping in any space available. The ground was littered with the green heat signatures of bodies of living, breathing humans.

"There must be hundreds," Pitbull reported.

"Maybe even thousands," Diesel agreed. "But we have to get in."

"Then we'd better make our move before the sun comes up," Big Jake advised.

Already, the eastern sky had lightened to a dark gray. The sun would rise within the next hour, and they'd be exposed to the mass of people surrounding the white tent.

Diesel squared his shoulders, handed Big Jake the night vision goggles and took a step forward. "Let's do this."

The team moved forward. While three provided cover, the other three bound, eating the distance thirty yards at a time, swinging wide to the rear of the encampment.

When they were within one bound of the white tent, they paused to regroup and plan their next move.

The light of dawn continued to push the black and gray of night toward the western sky, filling the horizon with rose gold and orange hues. They only had moments before the entire camp was awake and they would have missed their opportunity to rescue Reese and Klein.

"Uh, folks, we might have bigger problems than we thought," Big Jake said into Diesel's headset.

Diesel tensed as the meaning of Big Jake's warning became clear.

Chapter Thirteen

"Reese," a voice came to her in her sleep.

She blinked open her eyes and wondered if she'd really opened her eyes or was still asleep. The darkness was so profound, she couldn't even make out shapes.

"Reese," that same voice said. Only now she knew her eyes were open and the voice had to be that of Ferrence Klein, lying on the ground beside her.

"Ferrence?" she whispered.

"I got my hands loose," he said.

Any lingering fatigue vanished, and Reese bolted upright to a sitting position. "Do mine," she urged, feeling her way in the darkness toward him.

His hands touched her fingers and settled on the knot securing her wrists. For what felt like forever, he worked at the strap. Finally, he managed to slip one end through the knot, and the band fell away.

Her heart skipped beats as she worked the bindings at Ferrence's ankles. When they were both completely free, she rose to a squatting position.

Without light to see, she'd potentially walk over Jean-Paul and awaken him. This thought led to an important question: Should she free him, as well? Or should she focus on getting herself and Ferrence out of the camp and back to safety?

The president had been so certain his troops would find and free him. Had he changed his mind?

"President Sabando?" Reese felt her way to a lump on the tent floor.

"You're wasting time," Ferrence said sharply. "He wasn't willing to risk a run for it last night. Why should he do it now?"

"He's as much a prisoner as us. I can't just leave him here," Reese said. "Sir."

The man emitted a soft curse in French, and then mumbled in English, "What is it?"

"Do you want us to untie you?" she asked.

"You foolish girl," he said, his voice husky from sleep. "If you attempt to escape, you won't get out of this camp alive."

"Nevertheless, we have to try," she said. "This is your last chance."

He sighed. "Yes, I would wish you to untie me, so that I might face my brother in dignity."

Feeling the seconds ticking away at an alarming speed, Reese worked at the knot on Jean-Paul's wrists, while listening for sounds of the camp awakening. Already, the darkness was graying into predawn and she could make out shadowy shapes in the tent's interior. Dawn would bring the camp alive, and any chance of escape would be gone.

Just when she thought she couldn't get the knot untied, the end of the rope pushed through, and the binding fell away. When she started to rise to her feet, Reese was stopped by a hand on her arm.

"They will kill you if you try to escape," Jean-Paul said. "Let me negotiate your release. I would not like for a visitor to my country to leave in a funeral procession."

"We can't bank on your brother's good nature. Not after what happened in Kinshasa," Klein whispered. "You can't guarantee our safety."

Jean-Paul sighed and pushed to his feet, massaging his wrists where the rope had rubbed them raw. "I understand your hesitation." He held his hands out. "I wish you well in your pursuit of freedom."

Reese moved to the door of the tent and pushed aside the flap just enough to peer through the opening into the soupy gray of predawn.

Already, people were moving, if not awakening. A guard lay across the entrance to the tent, blocking her path. She would have to go over him or make another exit out the back. Closing the flap, she tiptoed to the opposite end of the tent. The darker gray lump lying over the other end indicated another guard sleeping at the back. Then she spotted a rip in the canvas at the base of the right side of the shelter.

Reese knelt on the ground, took both sides of the rip and pulled gently, easing the opening higher, trying to minimize the sound of ripping canvas. When she had the tear three feet high, she waved for Ferrence. "It's now or never."

He nodded.

Reese popped her head out. The predawn light was enough for her to determine there were no guards on this side. She slipped through the opening and made her way to the back, where the guard lay sleeping soundly, his weapon lying in his lap, his chin dropped to his chest. Beyond him was a jumble of brush and trees. If they could make it to that bunch of bushes, they might have a chance at escape. Reese glanced back.

Ferrence had his head through the gap.

She waved for him to join her.

When he had, she whispered. "You go. I'll hang back and make sure the guard doesn't wake and decide to start shooting."

Ferrence nodded, drew in a deep breath and tiptoed past the guard, toward the brush in the distance.

Before he was halfway there, a loud clanging sound ripped through what was left of the night.

The guard beside Reese jerked awake, his hands tightening around his rifle.

Reese could tell the exact moment he saw Ferrence by the way the sleeping man rolled to his feet and shouted something in Lingala.

Reese performed a side kick to the man's middle. She hit him so hard, he flung his weapon as he pitched to one side and landed hard, jolting his head against the ground. Reese pounced on the man, grabbed his arm and wrenched it up between his shoulders.

When she looked up, Ferrence had stopped halfway to the tree line.

"What are you waiting for? Go!" she shouted.

Instead, he lifted his hands in surrender.

Reese wanted to shake the man, but she had her hands full of the guard, squirming beneath her. Why didn't he run? He could get away. She'd find a way to get free and catch up to him.

Then she spotted a familiar figure coming up from behind Klein, running toward him with a rifle in his hands.

"Diesel?" she whispered, her heart flooding with hope and relief. He'd found her. Five other men appeared around him.

But they weren't the only ones. Dozens of people emerged from the woods. Emaciated men, women and children hurried toward the camp from every direction, including the tree line. Small children clambered around the legs of the SEALs, hands held out, begging in a language Reese could not understand.

Diesel and his men couldn't take a step without bumping into a child or a woman with his or her hand held out in piteous need.

Another clanking sound filled the air, and the men, women and children abandoned the

SEAL team and continued toward the center of camp.

They swarmed the camp like ants, their arms and legs so skinny, Reese couldn't fathom how they held them upright.

Before Diesel and his men could reach her, men carrying rifles emerged from around the tent and pointed their weapons at Ferrence and Reese. They shouted in Lingala.

Another voice shouted in English, "Put down your weapons, or we will kill the Americans."

Diesel ground to a halt, hesitated a moment, probably gauging whether he had half a chance to shoot the guards and get to Reese. More guards surrounded Reese in that moment of his hesitation, all pointing weapons in her direction.

Forced to release her prisoner, Reese pushed away from him and stood, her chin held high, her mouth set in a firm line, her heart racing. She prayed her captors wouldn't open fire.

"I should have guessed you would try to escape," Lawrence's voice sounded behind her. "I've heard from my sources you are a determined woman, who is not easily imprisoned, and that you have a team of men at your disposal."

"Don't hurt Mr. Klein," Reese said. "It was my idea to escape, not his."

"I have no intention of hurting either one of you, or these men who so foolishly thought they would rescue you." He tilted his head toward the camp. "In fact, to show you I am serious, they can keep their weapons, as long as they promise not to shoot me or my men." Lawrence raised his brows, giving Diesel a pointed stare.

"We won't shoot, if you won't shoot," Diesel promised.

Lawrence nodded. "So be it." He lifted a hand and said something in Lingala. His guards lowered their weapons, though they didn't appear happy about it.

Diesel and his men relaxed their holds on their rifles and came forward.

"Mr. Klein, I brought you and my brother here to see for yourselves what greed and corruption is doing to the people of our great nation." He swept his hand to the side. "Come." Lawrence waved to the SEALs. "You, too, will benefit from what you will see."

Reese waited for Diesel to join her, and

then walked with Lawrence to where a guard held his brother at gunpoint.

Lawrence touched the man's weapon and gave him a low, brief command. The man stepped back, pointing his rifle at the ground.

"You might think my methods were extreme, but what you will witness is a different kind of extreme." Lawrence swept his arm wide. "Behold the men, women and children of our country." Lawrence lifted his head and gazed at the swarm of people lining up in front of a giant cauldron.

A man, using a long wooden paddle, stirred a mash of some kind of grain in the cauldron, barely heating it before ladling out portions into the bare, dirty hands of those waiting. Men, women and small children took what they were given and licked their fingers clean of possibly the only nourishment they would receive that day.

"What is this?" Jean-Paul asked. "You have brought me to see people eating?"

"I've brought you to see the people employed in our country's mines—people who are more or less enslaved from the misfortune of their births, until the day they die." Lawrence's brows furrowed. "Look at them. Men our age reduced to skin and bone. Women who can't feed their children. Children who must work for the food they receive. They dig with their hands, carry bags of dirt and minerals heavier than their own weight, and die in the heat and humidity, their bellies empty." Lawrence drew in a deep breath and let it out. "This is your legacy, my brother."

Reese's heart squeezed in her chest when a toddler with the distended belly of the malnourished, missed his portion because he couldn't hold his little hands together.

The mush plopped to the ground. The little boy scooped up what he could, dirt and all, before he was pushed out of the way.

Reese wanted to gather the child in her arms and feed him as he should be fed.

"I do not approve of these conditions," Jean-Paul said.

Lawrence snorted. "But you allow them to be. When was the last time you visited a mine?"

"I visited one last year." Jean-Paul's frown mirrored his brother's. "These were not the conditions I witnessed."

"The people you employed to run the mine showed you what you wanted to see, not the truth," Lawrence said. "Now that you've seen reality, what do you plan to do about it? Surely you realize now why the people want a democratic election. They are tired of their needs being ignored. Tired of their children dying in mines when they should be going to school. Our country will not move into the twenty-first century at the rate we are killing our people."

Jean-Paul pounded his fist into his palm. "There will be change."

Lawrence crossed his arms over his chest. "Starting with allowing the election?"

Jean-Paul scrubbed a hand down his face and nodded. "Starting with the election. But understand, brother, there are factions who would rather take this country by force and keep it stirred up and fighting from within."

"These people cannot go on as they are," Reese whispered.

"You think I want them to?" Jean-Paul demanded.

Diesel cupped Reese's arm. "The working conditions are deplorable."

"It's all they have. Without this work and what little food they receive, they have nothing," Lawrence said. "The problem cannot be resolved by banishing them from the mines."

"I will do what I can until the election," Jean-Paul swore. "In the meantime, we must get more food to these people. I will work on a program to get the children out of the mines and into schools."

Lawrence turned to Ferrence. "I know you are here to negotiate interest in our country's natural resources to include the products of this mine. If you are truly interested in securing access to our treasures, you must be willing to invest in the infrastructure that will provide jobs for our people, not the kind that employs our children."

Reese held her breath, wondering what her client would say about what he'd seen. *Would he continue to be the privileged rich-man's son, concerned only about his own well-being, or would he be the man and diplomat he needed to be?*

Ferrence nodded. "Although I can't condone your method of bringing us here, I understand your desire to shed light on the situation. I will convey your message to my father and will work to insure we will help, not exacerbate the problem."

"That is all I ask," Lawrence said.

"My brother," Jean-Paul stepped forward. "What is in this for you? Do you wish to take my place as president of the Democratic Republic of the Congo?"

Lawrence shook his head. "If that were to happen, I would do my best for all of my people. But that is not why I brought you here. I brought you here because I could not allow this to continue. I have nightmares about the children I've seen die in the mud and dirt, just trying to work enough to be fed." He shook his head again.

Reese pressed a hand to her growling belly, her own hunger almost an embarrassment in light of the mine workers' plight. They needed food, clothing and shelter—the very basics of human needs.

The thump-thump of rotor blades whipping the air drew Reese's attention to an incoming helicopter.

"Your transportation back to Kinshasa has arrived." Lawrence stepped back to glance at the aircraft as it hovered over a bare spot on the ground. As it descended toward the ground, a loud bang ripped through the air.

The fuselage of the chopper exploded, sending the craft reeling to the side.

People screamed and ran to get out of the way of the blades as they hit the ground, broke off and were shot through the air.

Automatic weapon fire sounded from the direction of the road. Several trucks filled with men carrying rifles and rocket-propelled grenade launchers raced toward the camp.

"Get down!" Diesel yelled.

Bullets sprayed the dirt near Reese's feet. For a moment, she froze, not sure what was going on, or where she should run.

Diesel curled his arm around Reese and herded her toward a rise in the ground. He shoved her behind the berm and touched his hand to his ear. "Report." He listened for a moment and then responded. "Get the Sabandos and Klein to cover. I'll lay down suppressing fire until you're ready."

Diesel stretched out on the ground and aimed his rifle toward the men leaping from the backs of the trucks. He popped off several rounds. With each shot, he took out a rebel fighter. The men rushed toward them, more bodies than Diesel could fend off with just one rifle.

Soon, his shots were joined by others. The SEALs moved into defensive positions, forming a line, along with Lawrence's guards.

Reese kept her head low, feeling defenseless, unable to contribute to their survival.

One of the men who'd piled out of the back of the second truck took cover behind the truck. He carried what appeared to be a rocket-propelled grenade launcher. The man lifted the weapon to his shoulder.

"Holy hell." Reese touched Diesel's shoulder and pointed. "That man's going to fire an RPG."

Diesel redirected his aim to the rebel fighter as he shifted the weapon to his shoulder.

Reese held her breath, praying the rocket wouldn't launch before Diesel had a chance to take out the operator.

Diesel squeezed the trigger, hitting the man in the chest. He fell forward. His hand must have been on the trigger, because the RPG launched, hit the ground in front of him and exploded into a fiery blaze that shook the ground. The explosion pierced the truck's fuel tank, sending fuel spewing over the nearby fighters.

The battle had barely begun when it ended, but Reese couldn't remember a more intense fifteen minutes in her entire life.

The few remaining rebel fighters turned and ran for the woods.

Lawrence's guards gave chase.

When the dust and smoke settled, the SEALs rose from their positions.

Reese glanced around, taking a headcount before she let go of the breath she hadn't released since she'd started counting. All six SEALs were alive and unharmed. Klein hesitantly pushed to his feet, along with Jean-Paul and Lawrence Sabando.

"You see," Jean-Paul said, more calmly than one would have expected after the gunfire, "there are factions who would take what they can." He walked to the two abandoned trucks and stared down at the dead men scattered around. He nudged one of the men with the toe of his shoe. "At least one of their leaders is now accounted for."

Reese rose from her position and stood beside Diesel. He took her hand and led her to where Jean-Paul and Lawrence stood beside the dead man.

She recognized the man with the scar across his right cheek. "That's the man who kidnapped me and Mr. Klein," she said.

"Bosco Mutombo," Lawrence confirmed.

The DRC president shot a glance toward Ferrence. "What is this?"

Reese and Ferrence met gazes.

Ferrence nodded and looked directly into the president's eyes. "We didn't tell you about the incident because you had enough on your mind with the conference. And we came out of it all right."

The president looked around at the SEALs. "I take it your friends assisted your escape?"

Ferrence nodded.

"Do I want to know what qualifies them to assist in your liberation and our battle today?" President Sabando asked, his brows furrowing.

Reese and Ferrence shook their heads.

The president studied Diesel and his team for a moment, his eyes narrowing. Finally, he snorted. "Americans."

"Well, from my perspective, we would not have survived without them." Lawrence strode to Big Jake and held out his hand. "How can we send our thanks?"

Big Jake shook the man's hand and let go. "We'd prefer you didn't."

Lawrence nodded. "Brother, does this convince you that Mutombo's men were not working with me?"

Jean-Paul drew in a deep breath. "It does."

"And, having seen the wretched conditions of the mining operations, do you see the need for change?"

The DRC president frowned in the direction of the able-bodied miners who were headed into the mines to work. "I don't like it when I don't know what's going on in my country. But it appears I have missed a lot. As far as I'm concerned, your rescuers were never here and my military succeeded in removing one of our country's greatest enemies."

"With Bosco out of the picture, we will no longer waste resources on hunting him." Lawrence stared down at the dead man, and then looked out at the mining camp, where some people tended to the wounded before getting back to work. "We should be able to concentrate on helping our people."

The president followed his brother's gaze. "And we will." Then he faced Reese and Ferrence. "For now, perhaps our guests would like to return to Kinshasa?"

Lawrence glanced at the crashed helicopter. "Unfortunately, that helicopter was our transportation."

"I can have the presidential helicopter here in a few hours," the president said. "All I need is a telephone."

"President, sir," Diesel stepped forward. "My men have transportation waiting for us at the Kamenbe Airport. However, I would like to accompany Mr. Klein and Miss Brantley back to Kinshasa with you, if that's possible."

Jean-Paul nodded. "With my brother's approval, I will send my men to accompany your men and see to it you don't run into any other rebel fighters."

Big Jake held out his hand. "Mr. President, we'll see you back in Kinshasa."

President Sabando shook the man's hand. "We will be there before nightfall."

The three hours it took for President Sabando's helicopter to arrive gave those who remained ample time to tour the mining camp and take stock of the deplorable conditions.

By the time they loaded into the helicopter, the president had put in an order to deliver food and provisions to the site. He made arrangements to make unscheduled visits to other mining sites in the near future and sent word to his cabinet members to move forward with preparations for the election to take place on schedule.

Reese was able to settle back in her seat beside Diesel. With her hand held tightly in his, she slept all the way back to the capital city, putting off thought of what would happen next. She didn't want to think of leaving Diesel and never seeing him again.

Chapter Fourteen

Diesel loved the way Reese leaned her head on his shoulder and felt safe enough to fall asleep against him. He wished he could have slept as she did. Instead, his entire body was tense with thoughts of having to leave Reese soon.

At most, he'd be in Kinshasa long enough to see Reese and Klein on to the first airplane out of the country, which could be as soon as the next day. That gave him only one more night with Reese. One night to cram a lifetime of memories.

He couldn't believe he'd known her for just a few days. But those few days might as well have been a lifetime. Deep in his heart, he knew she was the woman for him. But did they have a chance in hell of making a relationship work? Hell, did she even feel as strongly as he did about her? Yes, he could bring her body to life, but body and heart were two different things.

Lawrence Sabando assured the president he'd released the dignitaries he'd herded into the van back in Kinshasa, shortly after they'd been taken away. None of them were harmed. His actions and those of his supporting fighters had been designed to frighten more than harm the people of the conference. He'd only wanted to make a statement that would be heard around the world and draw attention to the plight of the people of the DRC.

Lawrence couldn't promise his brother he'd go free after what he'd done, but he would work to insure his brother's safety.

Diesel had listened to the brothers speaking in English. The president had news that the rebellion in the city had been brought to order. By the time they landed on the grounds of the Palais de la Nation, where the president of the DRC lived, the city was calm, and people were back to their normal work and routines.

"You are welcome to stay here for the night," President Sabando offered. "But my driver is on standby and can take you wherever you would like to go."

For once, Ferrence looked to Reese first.

"I'd like to go back to the hotel. My luggage is there," Reese said.

Ferrence's brows dipped. "I too would like to go back to the hotel, as long as it's safe."

The president nodded. "My people assure me the uprising has been dealt with and the city center is back to normal. I will order the car around."

"Thank you."

The president's brows rose. "Mr. Klein, do you still wish to have the meeting with me?"

Ferrence's lips pressed into a thin line. He glanced from Jean-Paul to his brother, Lawrence. "Mr. President, I would love to, but I believe you have your hands full with the needs of your country. I won't deter you from taking care of your people first."

Diesel could have been gobsmacked. After all of Klein's determination to get a meeting with the president of the DRC, it shocked Diesel that the man declined—and politely, too.

Both the president and his brother nodded.

"Thank you for understanding," Lawrence said.

"I will put in a good word for you with my successor," the president offered.

"Thank you." Ferrence drew in a deep breath. "Please, don't let us keep you."

One of the president's assistants hurried out onto the lawn. Moments later, Reese, Diesel and Klein were ushered to the drive, where a long white limousine awaited them.

Shortly after, they were deposited at the entrance to the hotel.

"Allow me." Diesel scooped Reese up into his arms and carried her into the hotel. They stopped at the desk for key cards to their rooms. The hotel staff was apologetic about the events of the day before and offered to send a bottle of wine to their rooms, which they gladly accepted.

"If it's all the same to you, I'll call down for room service rather than go to dinner," Ferrence said, as they rode the elevator up to their floor.

"Good, because I don't think I can go another step," Reese said, her arm looped around Diesel's neck. She gave him a pointed glance. "However, I can stand on my own two feet."

"I know," he said with a smile. "But there might be broken glass or something sharp in the carpets."

"We're standing on tile," she pointed out with a smile.

"Humor me, will ya? I'm trying to be a gentleman. I don't get much practice."

Klein shook his head. "I'll arrange for our flights to leave tomorrow, and then I think I'll call my wife."

Reese's smile faded. "If we aren't meeting with the president, we really have no reason to stay." Her voice trailed off. Though she had answered Klein, her gaze met Diesel's.

Diesel's heart sank to the pit of his belly. Tomorrow was finally coming, the day he'd have to say goodbye to Reese. His arms tightened around her. If he could make the night last forever, he would.

The elevator arrived at their floor. Klein waved Diesel through first. The walk down the hallway to their rooms was accomplished in silence. At their doors, Diesel final set Reese on her feet.

Diesel held out his hand for Klein's key card.

For once, the man didn't argue. He handed over the card and waited in the hallway, while Diesel made a quick perusal of his suite.

Nothing seemed out of place or disturbed. In fact, the hotel staff had cleaned and made the bed. Everything was as it should be. When Diesel came out, he handed over the card. "You're still a target. If you need to leave your room for any reason, let me know. I'll go with you."

Klein nodded. "Thank you. You and your team have been invaluable to this event. I'll be sure to put in a good word for you."

Diesel's lips twisted. "We were never here."

Klein's mouth turned up on the corners, and he nodded. "Right. Then, I'll see you two in the morning, for the ride to the airport."

Klein entered his room, closed the door and locked it.

Alone at last, Diesel turned to Reese. "This is it."

Reese nodded. "Our last night together." She ran the card over the reader and opened the door. "I don't know what I would have done without you." She stepped across the threshold.

Diesel followed and closed the door behind him. Then he took her hand, spun her around and clamped her body to his. "Let's make this night count."

She laughed, the sound ending on what could only be a sob. "Damn right, we will."

"But it won't be our last," he said, as he lowered his mouth to hers."

"No? But, I'm leaving tomorrow," she whispered against his lips. "I won't see you again."

"But that's only tomorrow." He touched her lips with his in a feather-soft brush. "We'll be back in the States soon."

"And?" Reese reached for the hem of Diesel's shirt and dragged it up his body and over his head, and then tossed it to the floor.

"And, though I'm stationed out of Mississippi, I have a car. I can hop on a plane." He ran his fingers through her hair and cupped the back of her head. "I'm coming to see you." Then he kissed her and slid his hands down her neck and into the lapel of her suit jacket. With little effort, and a little help from her, he had that jacket on the floor in seconds.

Reese laid her hand along the side of his face and sighed. "Long-distance relationships never work." She reached for the button on his trousers and worked it free, and then dragged the zipper down ever so slowly.

With his body on fire, and his need for her rising with every move she made, Diesel fought back the urge to pound his chest like an eight-hundred-pound gorilla. She was special, and he needed to show her just how special she was. "Then I'll ask for a transfer to Virginia. It's closer to DC." He frowned. "Come to think of it, I don't even know where you live."

She shrugged. "I can live practically anywhere they have a need for bodyguards. Do they need them in Mississippi?"

"Only to fight off the alligators." He tugged the blouse from the waistband of her skirt and pulled it up over her head.

Reese raised her arms. "Alligators?"

"Yes. We train on the river and in the swamps. There are snakes and alligators."

Reese shivered. "Are they as bad as the crocodiles here in the Congo?"

Diesel shook his head, released the button on the back of her skirt and dragged her skirt down over her hips. "And there are no gorillas in Mississippi."

Reese's skirt fell to the floor.

Diesel slid his hands from her waist over her hips to cup the backs of her thighs. Then he lifted her, wrapping her legs around his waist. "Unfortunately, there's probably not much use for bodyguards, unless your client is having a Bubba feud with his neighbor.

But Mississippi is probably a lot safer than here." He kissed her long and hard before he broke it off and sighed. "Please tell me your next assignment isn't to Africa."

Reese chuckled and held on as he carried her through the bedroom and into the bathroom. "I don't even know if I'll have another assignment. Not after all that's happened here in the DRC."

"You'll be overwhelmed with work." Diesel set her on her feet beside the shower and tucked a strand of her hair behind her ear. "But do me a favor and save a little time for me."

"Really?" she asked, her eyes wide, shining with a layer of moisture. "Because I'm willing to give this long-distance thing a go, if you are." She brushed her thumb across his lips. "You see, I kind of like having a knight in shining armor swoop in to rescue me."

"Heck, I know you. You're perfectly capable of taking care of yourself, but please promise me you won't take on any more assignments in the jungle."

She shook her head. "I can't make any promises I can't keep. What if my next assignment takes me to the wilds of Costa Rica or Honduras?"

Diesel's fingers tightened on her arms. "I'll be crazy with worry."

"What if you are sent back to Afghanistan or Syria? I'll be nuts with worry."

"So, you care?"

She frowned. "Damn right, I do." She clasped his cheeks in both hands. "You don't get dragged through the jungle by a sexy man and not come out without forming some sort of attachment."

"Attachment, is it?" He liked the sound of that. "However we make it happen, promise me you'll see me again when we get back."

"That I can promise. If you can't come to me, perhaps we could meet halfway." She tipped her head. "What's that, someplace in Georgia?"

Diesel gathered her close, crushing her body to his. "We have the entire night to ourselves. No rebels, no teammates, no bosses. Just you and me, babe. Make love with me."

"Now you're talking." She wrapped her arms around his neck and pulled his head down so that she could meet his kiss with the fierceness that Diesel had learned he loved about this amazingly strong woman.

If they only had the night, he would make it the best night of their lives. But he wasn't ready to say goodbye. And he wouldn't. He'd find a way to see her again, stateside.

In the meantime, he had a job to do. He had a woman to please, and he wasn't going to waste a single minute he had with her.

He scooped her up into his arms and carried her into the shower, where they would begin their long night of forever.

* * * * *

Get 4 FREE REWARDS!

We'll send you 2 FREE Books
plus 2 FREE Mystery Gifts.

Harlequin® Romantic Suspense books feature heart-racing sensuality and the promise of a sweeping romance set against the backdrop of suspense.

FREE
Value Over
$20

YES! Please send me 2 FREE Harlequin® Romantic Suspense novels and my 2 FREE gifts (gifts are worth about $10 retail). After receiving them, if I don't wish to receive any more books, I can return the shipping statement marked "cancel." If I don't cancel, I will receive 4 brand-new novels every month and be billed just $4.99 per book in the U.S. or $5.74 per book in Canada. That's a savings of at least 12% off the cover price! It's quite a bargain! Shipping and handling is just 50¢ per book in the U.S. and 75¢ per book in Canada*. I understand that accepting the 2 free books and gifts places me under no obligation to buy anything. I can always return a shipment and cancel at any time. The free books and gifts are mine to keep no matter what I decide.

240/340 HDN GMYZ

Name (please print)

Address   Apt. #

City   State/Province   Zip/Postal Code

Mail to the **Reader Service**:
IN U.S.A.: P.O. Box 1341, Buffalo, NY 14240-8531
IN CANADA: P.O. Box 603, Fort Erie, Ontario L2A 5X3

Want to try two free books from another series? Call 1-800-873-8635 or visit www.ReaderService.com.

Get 4 FREE REWARDS!

We'll send you 2 FREE Books plus 2 FREE Mystery Gifts.

Harlequin Presents® books feature a sensational and sophisticated world of international romance where sinfully tempting heroes ignite passion.

FREE
Value Over
$20

YES! Please send me 2 FREE Harlequin Presents® novels and my 2 FREE gifts (gifts are worth about $10 retail). After receiving them, if I don't wish to receive any more books, I can return the shipping statement marked "cancel." If I don't cancel, I will receive 6 brand-new novels every month and be billed just $4.55 each for the regular-print edition or $5.55 each for the larger-print edition in the U.S., or $5.49 each for the regular-print edition or $5.99 each for the larger-print edition in Canada. That's a savings of at least 11% off the cover price! It's quite a bargain! Shipping and handling is just 50¢ per book in the U.S. and 75¢ per book in Canada*. I understand that accepting the 2 free books and gifts places me under no obligation to buy anything. I can always return a shipment and cancel at any time. The free books and gifts are mine to keep no matter what I decide.

Choose one: ☐ **Harlequin Presents®**
　　　　　　　Regular-Print
　　　　　　　(106/306 HDN GMYX)

☐ **Harlequin Presents®**
　 Larger-Print
　 (176/376 HDN GMYX)

Name (please print)

Address　　　　　　　　　　　　　　　　　　　　　　　　　　　　　　　　Apt. #

City　　　　　　　　　　　　　State/Province　　　　　　　　　　　　Zip/Postal Code

Mail to the **Reader Service:**
IN U.S.A.: P.O. Box 1341, Buffalo, NY 14240-8531
IN CANADA: P.O. Box 603, Fort Erie, Ontario L2A 5X3

Want to try two free books from another series! Call **1-800-873-8635** or visit www.ReaderService.com.

*Terms and prices subject to change without notice. Prices do not include applicable taxes. Sales tax applicable in N.Y. Canadian residents will be charged applicable taxes. Offer not valid in Quebec. This offer is limited to one order per household. Books received may not be as shown. Not valid for current subscribers to Harlequin Presents books. All orders subject to approval. Credit or debit balances in a customer's account(s) may be offset by any other outstanding balance owed by or to the customer. Please allow 4 to 6 weeks for delivery. Offer available while quantities last.

Your Privacy—The Reader Service is committed to protecting your privacy. Our Privacy Policy is available online at www.ReaderService.com or upon request from the Reader Service. We make a portion of our mailing list available to reputable third parties that offer products we believe may interest you. If you prefer that we not exchange your name with third parties, or if you wish to clarify or modify your communication preferences, please visit us at www.ReaderService.com/consumerschoice or write to us at Reader Service Preference Service, P.O. Box 9062, Buffalo, NY 14240-9062. Include your complete name and address.

HP18

Get 4 FREE REWARDS!

We'll send you 2 FREE Books plus 2 FREE Mystery Gifts.

FREE
Value Over
$20

Both the **Romance** and **Suspense** collections feature compelling novels
written by many of today's best-selling authors.

Get 2 Free Books,

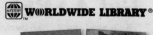

Plus 2 Free Gifts—

just for trying the
Reader Service!

WWLI7R2